喚醒你的英文語感！

Get a Feel for English !

喚醒你的英文語感！

Get a Feel for English !

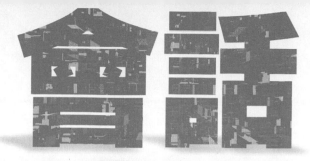

會話

留學課堂篇

第一手！海外求學應對手冊！

Conversation Boosters－Classes

- ☑ **240**個留學必備語彙
- ☑ **96**組對話開啟你與外國學生互動的談話頭
- ☑ **20**項遊戲規則立即融入西方學術殿堂

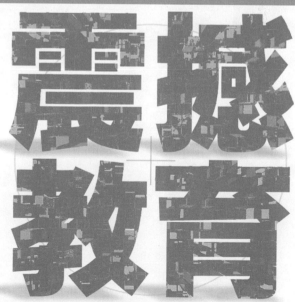

震撼教育

附 **2** 片伴讀CD

貝塔語言出版
Beta Multimedia Publishing

總編審◎王復國　　作者◎**Mark Hammons**

推薦序

萬事起頭難─留學 *101*

　　今日走在街上，迎面而來的很可能都是碩士或博士。自從台灣進入高科技時代，產業界對專業知識的要求提高不少，很多人因而都想出國深造，以為自己未來的職業生涯鋪路。從前國內學生要出國遇到的最大難題是財力證明；現在國人比較富有，錢不一定是最頭疼的問題。留學能否順利，如何適應、如何作好準備、如何不出差錯？這些問題對留學生來說都變得更重要。聰明的人都會想來點先前作業。

　　何邁（Mark Hammons）先生用他流暢而寫實的文筆，加上個人在美國讀書的經歷，以及多年來對台灣留學生的需求及期待的了解，特地將留學生涯分為八個重要議題來作動態介紹。每一個議題都可能是留學成敗的關鍵，也是台灣同學在國內接受高等教育過程中所不曾經驗過的。舉個例說，台灣的老師通常允許同學晚交作業或期末報告，但很多美國大學或研究所的老師卻不通融。台灣同學習慣了被動的受教模式，也很不容易適應美國大學課堂討論或做報告的主動發言方式。除此之外，還有課程編號的意義（像第二章 40 頁的 Psych 101）與台灣的大專院校的作法不一、測驗考試及做書面報告等要求也與國內的慣用模式不盡相同。何邁在各個單元中用簡短敘述及對話的方式介紹了真實的留學狀況、同學們關懷的議題、常用的相關單字片語等，這些都可以強化讀者的留學準備。而極為真實而生動、從留學生觀點出發的會話情境，更能讓讀者先體驗一下留學的真正滋味。

打從 1847 年清朝派遣第一位留學生容閎飄洋過海到耶魯大學深造開始，留學都是智慧的選擇，也是最划算的投資。台灣每年出國深造的人不少。大部分最後都能充實知識，滿載而歸，只有極少數的人會在異鄉遭逢滑鐵盧。主要原因都是缺乏相關資訊和事前作業不足。

　　A job well begun is half done. 相信你讀過本書後，對留學不會再陌生。

梁欣榮　2004.12.27

國立台灣大學外文系副教授

總編審序

　　莘莘學子遠渡重洋到了他鄉異地，為的是一圓求學深造的夢。辛苦的申請了學校與準備語言的考試，卻在進入了課堂才發現無所適從，難以融入正常的英語交談。雖然現今一般留學生的語言能力已經提昇許多，對國外的生活模式與文化也都耳熟能詳，在專業領域上的知識甚至可能早超越同儕，但縱使於課前下了不少功夫準備，卻仍無法在課堂上把自己的想法清楚、完善地表達出來。有此可見，用英語在課堂上說話、對談的能力在留學求學的過程中，是迫切需要的環節，但卻是不容易準備的。這也就是本書精選留學題材，作為英語會話學習的動機。

　　有幾個觀念要與準備留學的人分享。第一，語言考試的高分並不等於實際應付生活的語言能力，更不等於對異國文化的認知。要能真正融入課堂與老師同學互動，需要對該地／國之文化背景有相當程度的認識，也必須具備一些嘗試錯誤的勇氣。沒有開放的學習態度，語言能力是很難發揮出來的。第二，對語言的學習應是全面的，從簡單生字的正確使用，到片語的活用與語感的把握都是要學習揣摩的。本書的目的在於以模擬真實大學課堂中會遇到的典型難題，表現出最真實、最符合情境的對話，讓有意留學，或甚已在留學的人可以做好更萬全的準備。這些材料也可說是「學校沒有教我們的東西」，需要讀者多花心思去體會與練習。如能在觀念上先打通，你的留學之路就成功了一半。

本書設計理念

　　想與外國學生齊頭並進，就不能輸在起跑點上！儘管你自認 TOFEL 考得不錯，真正上起課來還是可能覺得趕不上別人。本書針對美國大學一學期內的各式課堂活動，實際上課情形，衍生出八個主題。分別介紹：

第一章　預告開學選課的競爭，並提供因應之道。

第二章　解讀課程大綱講義，徹底了解欲修得學分應盡的義務與享有的權利。

第三章　示範討論的技巧與思辯邏輯，以及如何在課堂上清楚表達自己的意見。

第四章　如何向教授討教，與求助助教的應答。

第五章　如何記筆記以及利用筆記的有效學習法。

第六章　分工合作做小組報告─如何善盡每個成員的優點與整合資源。

第七章　準備考試與應付英文試卷 all pass 秘笈。

第八章　寫 Essay 不可不知的英文文法與成規。

每章包括：

☞ **開學第一天**：對在學期中必須面對的課堂活動類型做基本概論簡介。

☞ **進入狀況**：實際例子的觀測解析。

☞ **討論 I、II**：針對實例而發展的討論對話，模擬與師生、同學互動，處理問題的應答。

☞ **補充單字 In Context**：提供更豐富高階的語彙，並以簡短對話套用釋義。

☞ **留學 Survival Kits**：提供與主題相關的資訊與解決文化差異的方法。

　　本書各單元的設計以語言難易度之差異循序漸進，並與學習情節發展環環相扣。每章各有主題，可依個人的需要，獨立學習。不管是留學美國或是英國，不管是教育制度或國情為何，本書所論及的學習領域與基本讀書方法，在你個人求學的過程絕都適用。

目錄 CONTENTS

Chapter

Class Registration

第 一 章

選課

☀️ 開學第一天

Are you ready? 先來一點新生訓練介紹，了解課程基本面……

Twenty years ago, class registration at some universities resembled an athletic event. You had to walk all over campus, from department to department, signing up in person for the classes you wanted. If you wanted to get into a popular course, you might have to run. And if you were a step too slow, you might not get in. These days, registration is not so grueling. For the most part, you can take care of it online. Most university web sites offer both a course catalog, which describes available classes, and a timetable, which gives specific information about times, instructors, and course availability.

　　二十年前，註冊選課在一些大學裡就好像一場運動會一樣。你得走遍整個校園，親自到各個系所去簽選你想上的課程。如果你想進入一門熱門的課程，你的手腳可得要快。如果你晚了一步，可能就進不去了。現今，註冊不再如此累人了。大部分的流程，你都可以在網上搞定。大部分的大學網站都有提供課程一覽表，說明所開設的課程內容，以及時間表，提供時間、授課者、和可選修課程的資訊。

進入狀況

📁 Course Catalog and Timetable 課程一覽表與時間表

English Dept. Course Descriptions

152 Intro to Shakespeare
1st Sem., 2nd Sem. and Summer Session; 3 cr.
Introduction to Shakespeare's best-known plays and their influence on other works of English and American literature. Open to Freshman.

221 The Bible as Literature
1st Sem.; 4 cr.
Introduction to the Bible. Selected readings from the Old and New Testaments and of English literature inflnenced by the Bible. Open to Freshmen.

English Dept Timetable

Course #	Course		Cr.	Notes and Prereqs.
102	Intro to American Lit.		4	• Section Required
Seats Open	**Time**	**Day**	**Place**	**Instructor.**
19	14:00	T, TH	333 Edu	Prof. King
Section	**Time**	**Day**	**Place**	**Instructor.**
102A	15:00	M, T	408 Edu	Kramer, S.
102B	16:00	T, W	408 Edu	Kramer, S.
102C	15:00	W, TH	203 Edu	Cossey, B.
102D	16:00	TH, F	203 Edu	Cossey, B.
Course #	**Course**		**Cr.**	**Notes and Prereqs.**
207	ESL: Academic Essays		3	• English Assessment Test required • 3Cr. On Eng. 101 • Not open to auditors
Seats Open	**Time**	**Day**	**Place**	**Instructor.**
12	9:55	MWF	129 Poe	Prof. Carney

Key

Sem.	= semester
Cr.	= credits
Prereqs.	= prerequisites

英文系課程說明

152 莎士比亞概論

第一學期，第二學期及暑期班；三學分

介紹莎士比亞最知名的劇本，以及它們對其他英美文學作品的影響。開放給大一新生選修。

221 聖經文學

第一學期；四學分

聖經概論。挑選新、舊約聖經中的章節，以及受聖經影響的英國文學作品。開放給大一新生選修。

英文系時間表

課程代號	課程		學分數	備註及先決條件
102		美國文學概論	4	• 需上分組課程

開放修課人數	時間	上課日	地點	授課者
19	14:00	二、四	333 Edu	金教授

組別	時間	上課日	地點	授課者
102A	15:00	一、二	408 Edu	S.克拉默
102B	16:00	二、三	408 Edu	S.克拉默
102C	15:00	三、四	203 Edu	B.科西
102D	16:00	四、五	203 Edu	B.科西

課程代號	課程	學分數	備註及先決條件
207	ESL: 學術論文	3	• 需做英文程度測驗
			• 修過三學分的英文 101
			• 不開放旁聽

開放修課人數	時間	課日	地點	授課者
12	9:55	一、三、五	129 Poe	卡尼教授

Sem. = 學期　　Cr. = 學分數　　Prereqs. = 先決條件

＊注意：套色部分為以下討論 I、II.對話內重複使用的字彙，並加上了音標註解。

討論 I.  ○○

CD1 03

📁 Signing up for Classes

It's the first week of classes, Peter and Cindy are trying to finalize their course schedules.

Peter: So [1] <u>what are you taking</u> this semester?

Cindy: Do you mean "Which classes did I want to take?" or "Which ones did I [2] <u>get into</u>?"

Peter: Did you try to get into Clarke's course on essay writing?

Cindy: Yeah, I tried. Forget about it. He only takes 17 students.

Peter: I know. That class [3] <u>filled up</u> weeks ago. Now there's a [4] <u>waiting list</u> about a mile long.

Cindy: I did get into American Literature though.

Peter: How did you [5] <u>manage</u> that?

Cindy: It's a [6] <u>required class</u> for English majors. Since everybody needs to take it, they had to open up a new [7] <u>section</u>.

Peter: You're kidding! How'd you hear about that?

Cindy: I went in to [8] <u>talk with</u> the professor <u>in person</u>. I was about to beg him to let me in when he told me not to worry because he'd already added the new section.

Peter: [9] <u>When you say</u> section, <u>do you mean</u> discussion section?

Cindy: Yes, everybody goes to the same big [10] <u>lecture</u>, but there are three or four discussion sections.

📁 選課

上課的第一週。彼得和辛蒂正試著排定他們的課程表。

彼得：那妳這學期修了什麼課？
辛蒂：你是指我想修哪些課，還是我選進了哪些課？
彼得：妳有沒有嘗試去選克拉克的論文寫作那門課？
辛蒂：有呀，我試過了。甭提了，他只收十七個學生。
彼得：我知道。那門課幾個禮拜前就滿了。現在連候補名單都已大排長
　　　龍了。
辛蒂：不過我選到了美國文學。
彼得：妳是怎麼辦到的？
辛蒂：這是英文系的必修課。因為每個人都得修那門課，他們只好開一
　　　個新的小組。
彼得：妳在開玩笑吧！妳怎麼知道那個消息的？
辛蒂：我親自去跟教授談。我正打算要求他讓我加入那門課，他就叫我
　　　別擔心，因為他已經加開了一個新的小組。
彼得：妳說「小組」，妳是指討論小組嗎？
辛蒂：是的，每個人都要去同一個大班級上課，不過會有三或四個討論
　　　小組。

 ○。

1. **What are you taking?** 你修哪些課？

2. **get into** 選進

3. **fill up** 滿

4. **waiting list** [ˈwetɪŋ ˌlɪst] *n.* 候補名單

5. **manage** (to do sth.) 設法（做……）

6. **required class** [rɪˈkwaɪrd ˈklæs] *n.* 必修課

7. **(discussion) section** [(dɪˈskʌʃən) ˈsɛkʃən] *n.* 討論小組

8. **talk with sb. in person** 親自和某人談話

9. **When you say ... do you mean ...?**

   當你說……的時候，你是指……嗎？

10. **lecture** [ˈlɛktʃɚ] *n.* 講課

:::::: *Take a Break*

 ○。

CD1 04

📂 Getting into a Closed Class

Peter visits Professor King at his office to try to get into his American Literature class.

Peter: Professor King? [1] <u>Do you have a minute</u>?

King: Sure. How can I help you?

Peter: My name is Peter. I'm an English major. I'm interested in taking your course on American Literature. I heard a new section [2] <u>opened up</u>.

King: One did. Unfortunately, it filled up almost immediately.

Peter: I guess I was [3] <u>a step too slow</u>.

King: You could put your name on the waiting list. You'd be [4] <u>at the top of the list</u>.

Peter: OK, thanks. How likely do you think it is that I'd be able to get in?

King: I can't say for certain, but I wouldn't be surprised if a few students [5] <u>drop</u>. Usually a few do after they see how much reading they're going to have to do.

Peter: Really? I [6] <u>don't mind</u> reading a lot. I've already [7] <u>looked through</u> your [8] <u>syllabus</u> and I'm really interested in almost all of the authors.

King: Tell you what, Peter. Why don't you just come to the first few lectures? I'll put you on the waiting list. If anybody drops—and as I said, somebody probably will—you'll be in.

Peter: That sounds great. Thank you so much.

📁 加入已經結束選課的課程

彼得到金教授的辦公室拜訪他，設法要加入他美國文學的課。

彼得：金教授？能耽誤你一點時間嗎？

金　：當然。有什麼我能效勞的？

彼得：我叫彼得。我是英文系的學生。我對選修你那門美國文學的課程很有興趣。我聽說開了一個新的小組。

金　：的確是有一組。遺憾的是，幾乎馬上就被選滿了。

彼得：我猜想我晚了一步。

金　：你可以把名字放在候補名單上，你會是名單上的第一人。

彼得：好的，謝謝。你認為我能修到這門課的可能性有多高呢？

金　：我說不準，不過如果有一些學生退選我也不會很訝異的。通常有些人發現他們得讀那麼多的書之後，就會退選。

彼得：真的嗎？我不介意要讀很多書。我已經仔細看過了你的課程大綱，而且我對所有的作者幾乎都很有興趣。

金　：這樣吧，彼得。你何不前幾堂課就來上？我會把你放到候補名單上。如果有人退掉的話─正如我說的，有人可能會那麼做─你就能進來。

彼得：聽起來很棒。非常謝謝你。

○。

1　Do you have a minute? 能耽誤你一點時間嗎？

2　open up 開設

3　a step too slow 晚了一步

4　at the top of the list 名單上的第一人

5　drop [drɑp] v. 退選

6　don't mind 不在乎⋯⋯

7　look through 仔細看過一遍

8　syllabus [ˋsɪləbəs] n. 課程大綱

●●●●補充單字 In Context CD1 🎧 05

pass / fail 及格／不及格

Classmate:　I'm really having a hard time in this class, but I need it to graduate.

☞ You:　There is still time to switch and take it **pass / fail**. That way, you can still get the credits without having to worry about your grade.

同學：　我在這門課真的吃足了苦頭，不過我需要它才能畢業。

你：　現在還來得及把它換成過／不過制。如此一來，你仍然可以拿到學分，而且不用擔心你的成績。

（註：過／不過制指所選之課程只分及格（過）與不及格（不過），而不計分數高低。）

---

transcript 成績單

☞ You:　Two of the classes I took last semester haven't appeared on my **transcript**.

Official:　Have you tried looking on the second page?

你：　我有兩門上學期修的課沒有出現我的成績單上。

職員：　你有沒有試過在第二頁找一找？

honors / honors student 榮譽／榮譽生

Classmate: Are you taking this class for honors?

☞ You: No. I'm not an **honors student**.

同學：   你修這門課是為了要爭取榮譽學分嗎？

你：   不，我真可不是榮譽生。

instructor's consent 授課者的同意

☞ You: I need to get the **instructor's consent** to take Creative Writing 332.

Classmate: That's Professor Jones' class. She's pretty demanding.

你：   我需要得到授課者的同意才能選修創意寫作 332。

同學：   那是瓊斯教授的課。她的要求很高。

withdraw 退選

☞ **You:**　　Have you really decided to **withdraw** from all your courses?

　Classmate:　Yes. I hate college. I'm moving to Botswana to become a cattle herder.

你：　　你真的已經決定要把所有的課都退掉嗎？

同學：　是啊，我討厭大學。我要搬到波紮納去牧牛。

---

deadline 截止日期

☞ **You:**　　I'd like to drop my Physics class.

　Official:　I'm sorry. The **deadline** for dropping classes has passed.

你：　　我想退掉物理學的課。

職員：　很抱歉。退選的截止日期已經過了。

tuition 學費

Classmate: Have you paid your **tuition** yet?

☞ You: No. I'm waiting until right before the deadline.

同學：   你交學費了嗎？

你：   沒有。我要等到截止日期的前一天再交。

stay on top of sth. （在某事）保持出色的表現

☞ You: All these deadlines are driving me crazy.

Classmate: I know it. It's hard to **stay on top of every-thing**.

你：   這些截止日期都快把我逼瘋了。

同學：   我明白。要在每件事情上保持出色的表現是很難的。

late fee 滯納金

Official:	You can still register, but you'll have to pay a **late fee**.
☞ You:	OK. I don't know how I managed to miss the deadline.
職員：	你還是可以註冊，不過你必須繳滯納金。
你：	好的。我真不知道我是怎麼錯過截止日期的。

prerequisite 先決條件

☞ You:	Are there any **prerequisites** for English 303?
Professor:	Yes. You should have taken at least one introductory course on Shakespeare.
你：	修英語 303 這門課有沒有任何先決條件呢？
教授：	有的。你至少必須修過一門莎士比亞概論的課。

 留學 Survival Kits CD1 06

1 號 法 寶 Credits 學分

☞ In order to graduate from most colleges and universities, you need about 120 credits. That's 15 credits a semester for four years. Most schools require you to take 15 or 16 credits a semester in order to qualify as a full-time student. The tuition you've paid entitles you to take at least that many credits. Some students take a few extra credits, but most schools require you to seek special permission to take more than 20 credits. Graduate students normally take fewer credits because their courses are more demanding. Nine to twelve credits is considered a full load for a graduate student. As graduate students begin investing more time in their own research and writing, they take fewer and fewer credits.

You may also consider auditing a class — you won't receive credit, but you won't have to worry about receiving a grade, either.

☞ 要從大多數大專院校畢業，你需要大約一百二十個學分，也就是每學期修十五學分，修四年。多數的學校會要求你每學期要修十五到十六學分，以符合作為一個全職學生的資格。你所付的學費讓你至少得以修那麼多的學分數。有些學生會修額外的學分。不過大部分的學校會要求你先取得特殊的許可才能讓你修超過二十個學分。研究生通常會修較少的學分，因為他們的課程較為吃力。對研究生來說，九到十二學分被認為是上限。隨著研究生開始花更多時間在他們自己的研究和寫作上，他們修的學分數就會越來越少。

你也可以考慮去旁聽別的課程——你不會得到學分，不過你也不用擔心成績。

2 號 法 寶 **Getting In** 加選

☞ In order to get into the classes you want, the most important thing to do is plan ahead. You need to be aware of all the various deadlines and requirements. Be sure to take care of everything on time. That's step one. Step two is being a good student. Professors like to have smart, ambitious students in their classes. For certain classes — say a creative writing class, for example — you may have to submit a sample of your work for the professor to review. The better your work, the better your chances of getting in. For an extra edge, you can try making personal contact with a particular instructor. Even if you don't make it into a particular class, you might show up on the first day. Perhaps somebody will drop the class and a seat will open. Or you might make a good impression on the instructor and he or she might decide to let you in.

☞ 為了能進入你想上的課程，事先規劃是最要緊的。你需要知道所有
不同的截止日期和規定。要確保能準時將一切準備好。那是第一
步。第二步是做一個好學生。教授喜歡收聰明、具進取心的學生在
他們的班上。針對某幾門課——說創意寫作——你也許得交一篇範
例作品給教授過目。你寫得越好，就越有機會進入那門課。如果想
更佔優勢，你可以嘗試跟某位授課者私下聯繫。即使你沒能成功選
到某門課，你還是可以在上課的第一天出現。或許會有人退選，那
就會有空缺了。抑或你可能會給授課者一個好印象，而他或她也許
會決定讓你加選。

::::: *Quiz*

Complete the dialogue.

open up, lecture, manage, registering, at the top of, waiting list, required, drop, get into

Peter: Wow! 1_____ for classes can be as hard as taking them!

Cindy: Did you finally 2_____ to 3_____ all the classes you wanted?

Peter: All of them except American Literature. That's a 4 _____ class for English majors. I'm on a 5 _____ for that one.

Cindy: I'm sure a seat will 6_____. Somebody will 7_____.

Peter: Yeah, I bet they will. And I'm 8_____ the list.

Cindy: OK. So I'll see you at the first 9_____?

....

📁 Answers

1. registering   6. open up
2. manage   7. drop
3. get into   8. at the top of
4. required   9. lecture
5. waiting list

Notes

Chapter 2

Sample Syllabus

第 二 章

解讀課程大綱

開學第一天

Are you ready? 先來一點新生訓練介紹，了解課程基本面⋯⋯

After moving in to your dorm room or apartment, registering for classes, and buying your books, you're ready for the main event: your first day of classes. Once in class, the teacher will hand out a very important piece of paper: the syllabus for that class. Although each syllabus is a little different, they all contain information about the content of the course, the course requirements, and some basic information about how you will be graded.

　　搬入你的宿舍或是公寓、註冊選課和買書之後，你就已經準備好迎接最重要的一件事：頭一天上課。一旦開始上課，老師會發給你非常重要的一張紙：課程大綱。雖然每堂課的課程大綱不盡相同，但其中都會包含課程的內容、課堂要求、和一些基本的評分標準。

進入狀況

📁 Sample Course Syllabus 課程大綱範例

English 101 — Introduction to Academic Writing

Prof. Donald King   Kerr Hall 702   Tu./Thu. 9:30 — 11:00

Course Objectives

1. This class will provide instruction in writing first drafts, revising, and editing, as well as introduce basic concepts of English grammar, usage, and punctuation.
2. By the end of the semester, you should be able to organize and write a ten-page academic essay.
3. Students will learn to revise and edit their own work.

Required Books

A Writer's Reference, 4th ed., by Diana Hacker (1999, Bedford/St. Martin's); A Manual for Writers of Term Papers, Theses, and Dissertations, 6th ed., by Kate Turabian (1996, Chicago).

Requirements, Grading and Attendance

1. Students will write three take-home essays and two in-class essays. These will be submitted together in a portfolio at the end of the semester.
2. 80% of the final grade will be based on the average score of the five essays. 20% of the final grade will be based on participation in in-class discussions.
3. Students may choose to revise and resubmit two of their five essays.
4. 5% will be deducted from a student's final grade for each absence over three.
5. Any student who misses more than six classes will be given an N/C (no credit).

Student Conduct

Students should come to each class prepared to discuss the reading assignment for that day. All cell phones and pagers must be set to silent mode or turned off during class.

Getting assistance: Students with questions may see me during my office hours, on Wednesdays and Fridays from 2 to 4 at Wilson 205. The Writing Center is located in Cabel Hall Room 104, and is open from 9 a.m. to 9 p.m., seven days a week. The computer lab is open from 7 a.m. to 9:30 p.m., Monday to Friday.

英文 101 ─初級學術寫作

唐諾‧金 教授　　　　　　　凱爾樓 702 室　　　　　週二／四 9:30 ─ 11:00

課程目標

1. 本課程講授寫作之擬稿、修改和編輯，同時也介紹英文文法、慣用語和標點符號的基本概念。

2. 學期結束時，學生應該已具備組織並撰寫一份十頁學術報告的能力。

3. 學生將會學到如何修改、編輯自己的作品。

指定書目

寫作指南，第四版，戴安娜‧海克著（1999，貝福德/聖馬汀斯）；寫作手冊：如何撰寫學期報告、碩博士論文，第六版，凱特‧特拉邊著（1996，芝加哥）。

課堂要求、評分、出缺席

1. 學生將必須各在家中完成三篇、在課堂上完成兩篇文章，並且在學期末做成學習檔案一起繳交。

2. 這五篇文章的平均分數將佔期末成績的百分之八十。課堂討論的參與度則佔期末成績的百分之二十。

3. 學生可以從五篇文章中選兩篇作修改，並且重新繳交。

4. 超過三次缺席後每次從期末成績中扣百分之五的分數。

5. 任何學生缺席超過六堂課，則該門課程不給予學分。

學生表現

每次上課都要準備好討論當天指定的閱讀範圍。上課時所有的手機和傳呼器都必須設定為靜音模式或是關機。

尋求協助

有問題的學生可以在每星期三和星期五下午，於我辦公的時間：兩點到四點，到威爾森樓 205 室來找我。寫作教室位於坎貝爾樓 104 室，開放時間為早上九點到晚上九點，每日開放。電腦教室的開放時間為星期一到星期五的早上七點到晚上九點半。

＊注意：套色部分為以下討論 I., II. 對話內重複使用的字彙，並加上了音標註解。

 ○。

CD1 🎧 08

📂 Discussing the Syllabus

Peter and Cindy have just finished their first day of English 101.

Peter: Hey, Cindy. What did you think of the first day of English 101?

Cindy: I liked it pretty well, I guess. Professor King talks really fast, though. I had trouble understanding his explanation of the ¹syllabus.

Peter: I was impressed with the course ²objectives. By the end of the semester, we should be good at organizing and writing ³ten-page essays.

Cindy: I'm just a little worried about the writing ⁴portfolio that we have to turn in at the end of the semester. What's that all about?

Peter: I guess the professor wants to see all of our essays together—to see how much progress we've made during the ⁵term.

Cindy: So there are no ⁶midterms or ⁷finals for this class?

Peter: No, just the essays. Oh yeah, and we also get a grade for ⁸participation, so you'd better come to class prepared to discuss the reading.

Cindy: It sure sounds like a lot of work for just three ⁹credits ...

📂 討論課程大綱

彼得和辛蒂方剛上完英文 101 第一天的課程。

彼得：嘿，辛蒂。妳覺得第一天的英文 101 怎麼樣？

辛蒂：我想我還蠻喜歡的。不過金教授講話的速度太快了。我聽不太懂他對課程大綱的說明。

彼得：我對課程目標的印象深刻。在這學期結束前，我們得要有本事組織、撰寫一份十頁的報告。

辛蒂：我只是有點擔心我們期末要交的寫作學習檔案。那到底是什麼東西啊？

彼得：我想教授是想集中一次看我們所有的報告，看看這個學期之中我們進步了多少。

辛蒂：所以這門課沒有期中考跟期末考囉？

彼得：沒有，只要交報告。噢，對了，咱們還有一個課堂參與度的分數，所以妳來上課的時候最好已經準備好作閱讀討論。

辛蒂：聽起來為了這三個學分要做的事情可多了……

 ○。

1 **syllabus** [ˈsɪləbəs] *n.* 課程大綱

2 **objective** [əbˈdʒɛktɪv] *n.* 目標

3 **ten-page essay** 十頁的報告

4 **portfolio** [portˈfolɪˌo] *n.* 檔案

5 **term** [tɝm] *n.* 學期

6 **midterm** [ˈmɪdˌtɝm] *n.* 期中考

7 **final** [ˈfaɪn!] *n.* 期末考

8 **participation** [pɚˌtɪsəˈpeʃən] *n.* 參與

9 **credit** [ˈkrɛdɪt] *n.* 學分

:::::: *Take a Break*

 ○ ○

CD1 09

🗁 Getting Help on a Paper

A couple of weeks later Peter and Cindy meet in the school cafeteria. Cindy looks unhappy.

Peter: What's wrong, Cindy?

Cindy: I got a really bad grade on my first essay for English 101.

Peter: Why don't you [1] rewrite it and turn it in again?

Cindy: Yeah, right.

Peter: I'm serious, Cindy. It says right in the syllabus that you can rewrite two of your essays and [2] resubmit them.

Cindy: OK, yeah, I see that, right here in the [3] Requirements, [4] Grading and [5] Attendance section.

Peter: You should definitely do the rewrite. Remember Professor King said that [6] revision is the most important part of [7] the writing process.

Cindy: But what if I don't know how to improve my essay?

Peter: Why don't you ask Professor King for some advice? He has [8] office hours this afternoon.

Cindy: How do you know that?

Peter: Look in your syllabus. You could also go to the [9] Writing Center for help. They're really nice and very helpful.

📁 尋求協助寫報告

幾個星期過後，彼得和辛蒂在學校的自助餐廳碰面。辛蒂看起來不怎麼開心。

彼得：怎麼啦，辛蒂？

辛蒂：我的第一篇英文 101 報告拿了個很糟的成績。

彼得：你為什麼不重寫再交一次？

辛蒂：是－－噢。

彼得：我是認真的，辛蒂。課程大綱裡面寫得很清楚，妳可以重寫兩篇報告，並且再交一次。

辛蒂：好吧，對，我看到了，就列在課堂要求、評分、出缺席的部份。

彼得：妳真的應該重寫。記不記得金教授說過，修改是寫作過程中最重要的一個部分？

辛蒂：但是如果我不知道要如何改進我的報告呢？

彼得：妳何不向金教授請教看他有什麼建議呢？今天下午是他的辦公時間。

辛蒂：你是怎麼知道的？

彼得：看看妳的課程大綱。妳也可以去寫作教室求助。他們人很好而且很幫忙。

1 rewrite [ri`raɪt] *v.* 重寫，[`riraɪt] *n.* 重寫

2 resubmit [ri͵səb`mɪt] *v.* 重新遞交

3 requirement [rɪ`kwaɪrmənt] *n.* 課堂要求

4 grading [gredɪŋ] *n.* 評分

5 attendance [ə`tɛndəns] *n.* 出席（狀況）

6 revision [rɪ`vɪʒən] *n.* 修改

7 the writing process 寫作過程

8 office hours 辦公時間

9 writing center 寫作教室

●●● 補充單字 In Context CD1 10

elective 選修課

☞ You:　　　How many **electives** do you have this
　　　　　　semester?

Classmate:　I'm in my first year of Engineering school, so
　　　　　　I only have one.

你：　　　　這個學期你有幾門選修課？

同學：　　　這是我在工學院的第一年，所以只有一門課。

---

required course 必修課

Classmate:　What are you doing in this Philosophy class?
　　　　　　Aren't you a Physics major?

☞ You:　　　Yeah, but it's a **required course** for me.

同學：　　　你幹嘛來上這門哲學課呀？你不是物理系的嗎？

你：　　　　對呀，但這是我的必修課。

TA (teaching assistant) 助教

☞ You:　　　　How is your Spanish **TA**?

　　Classmate:　He's great! He even holds review sessions before each test to help us prepare.

　　你：　　　　你的西文助教怎麼樣？

　　同學：　　　棒極了！他甚至在每次考試前上複習課幫我們準備。

---

exceptions 例外

☞ You:　　　　The professor said late papers would not be accepted — no **exceptions**.

　　TA:　　　　I guess you'd better get started on them early, then!

　　你：　　　　教授說他不收遲交的報告——沒有任何例外。

　　助教：　　　那，我想你最好早點開始寫。

unexcused 無正當理由的

☞ You:	Is attendance required for this course?
TA:	Yeah, of course. The professor said that students with more than seven **unexcused** absences will be dropped from the course. No exceptions!

你：	這門課有規定不能缺席嗎？
助教：	是呀，當然。教授說超過七次無正當理由缺席的學生，這門課就會被當掉。沒有任何例外！

oral exam 口試

Classmate:	We have a ten-minute **oral exam** next Monday morning.
☞ You:	I know. Have you seen the list of potential topics yet?

同學：	我們下星期一有個十分鐘的口試。
你：	我知道。你看到列出可能會考的題目那張表了嗎？

evaluate 對……評價

Classmate: Professor Smith will **evaluate** our entire portfolio of assignments at the end of the semester before she gives us our final grade.

☞ You: Isn't class participation considered as well?

同學： 學期末的時候，在史密斯教授打總成績之前，她會先評我們學習檔案中所有作業的分數。

你： 課堂參與度不是也列入成績嗎？

---

curve 學生成績曲線

Classmate: I only got a 64 on my final exam, but I still got a B+.

☞ You: Why? Did the professor grade on a **curve**?

同學： 我期末考只考了 64 分，可是我還是得了個 B+。

你： 為什麼？教授是不是按照成績曲線來打等第？

assessment 評量

☞ You:　　　What's included in our final **assessment**?

Professor:　At the end of the term I will look at all of your papers, tests, and group presentations together.

你：　　　我們的期末評量包含了哪些項目？

教授：　　學期末的時候，我會看你們所有的書面報告、測驗分數、以及分組口頭報告。

---

policy 政策

☞ You:　　　What does this mean: "It is school **policy** to forbid the use of recording equipment in the classroom"?

Professor:　It means you can't tape the class.

你：　　　「學校的政策規定禁止在教室中使用錄音器材」，這句話是什麼意思？

教授：　　意思是你不能錄下上課的內容。

留學 Survival Kits  CD1 🎧 11

1 號 法寶 **English 101** 英語 101

☞ In American universities, classes are often numbered according to their level of difficulty. Introductory classes, often taken by 1st year undergraduates, are listed as 100-level courses. For example, Introduction to Psychology may be called Psychology 101, or Psych 101 for short. Classes at the 300 and 400 levels are more specialized, and are sometimes reserved for students majoring in that field.

☞ 在美國大學裡，課程通常會依照難度來編號。大學一年級生常修習
　　的概論課程通常列為程度 100 的課。例如，心理學概論可能就叫作
　　心理學 101（Psychology 101，或是簡稱 Psych 101）。程度
　　在 300 和 400 的課程則較為專業，而且有時只保留給主修該領域
　　的學生選修。

2 號 法 寶 **Teaching Assistants** TA，助教

☞ If you attend a large university, teaching assistants will play a large role in your education. Teaching assistants are typically graduate students who have been hired to help teach a subject within their area of expertise. A professor may deliver the main lecture, but if the class is large, teaching assistants usually lead the discussion groups and evaluate your performance on papers and tests. And they are typically more readily available should you need extra help or advice. Many TAs are excellent teachers. Others are not so excellent. But the same is true of professors. The best advice is to try to maximize the contact you have with the best teachers—whether they be professors or TAs or other students—and to minimize your contact with the duds.

☞ 如果你唸的是一所大型的大學，那麼助教在你的求學過程中將扮演極吃重的角色。助教通常是研究所的學生，他們被聘來協助教授其專業領域的科目。教授講授主要的課程，但是假使是一個大班級的話，助教通常會指導討論小組並且評估你的作業與考試表現。此外，當你需要額外的協助或建議時，他們通常較容易找得到人。許多助教都是很棒的老師，有一些就沒有那麼棒了。但是教授何嘗不是如此呢？最好的建議是要儘量增加與好老師的接觸——不論他們是教授、助教、或是其他同學——並且儘量將與爛老師的接觸減到最低。

3 號 法 寶   The Curve 成績分佈曲線

☞ The curve: either you love it or you hate it. When you are graded on a curve, your grade reflects how well you performed relative to the other students in your class. If you did better than most of them, you'll get a good grade and you'll love the curve. If most of them outperform you, you'll get a poor grade and you'll hate the curve. In general, grading on a curve is a method little loved by students. The competitive nature of the system means that only a few of your classmates will get the best grades. And the lowest grades will always be reserved for somebody. On the other hand, the curve does offer some protection for students. If your professor devises a test that is devilishly difficult, everyone in the class might score poorly. Perhaps the highest score will be a 67/100. But on a curve, the 67 would receive an A. Love it or hate it, the curve is a fact of life.

☞ 成績分佈曲線：你不是很喜歡就是很痛恨。當你是被按照成績分佈
曲線來評分時，你的成績反應出你跟班上其他同學比較後的表現。
如果你表現得比大多數的人好，你就會得到好成績，而且就會愛極
了成績分佈曲線。如果多數的人都贏過你，你就會得到很差的成
績，而且也會痛恨成績分佈曲線。一般說來，成績分佈曲線的評分
方式並不受學生歡迎。這種評分法的競爭性質意味著只有少數幾個
同學能得到最好的成績，而總是會有人會得到最低的成績。在另一
方面來說，成績分佈曲線卻提供了學生一些保障。假使教授出的考
題出奇地刁鑽，班上每個人的分數也許都會很低。總分一百分，或
許最高的成績只有六十七分。不過如果採用成績分佈曲線評分法，
那個考了六十七分的人會得到個 Ａ 。不管你喜不喜歡，成績分佈曲
線都是不可避免的現實。

::::: *Quiz*

Complete the dialogue.

**participation, ten-page essays, revisions, portfolio,
syllabus, rewriting, resubmit, writing center, due, credit**

Peter: How many essays are we supposed to include in our
1_____?

Cindy: I can't remember. Let's check in the 2_____.

Peter: It says five essays—three take-home and two in-class.
Uh-oh... our 3_____ are 4_____ next week!

Cindy: You didn't know that?

Peter: I've been too busy 5_____ the last essay.

Cindy: I know what you mean. Writing is hard work. I went to
the 6_____for help.

Peter: I'm glad we get some 7_____ for our 8_____
in class. Otherwise, I might get a big fat zero.

Cindy: Come on, Peter! Finish your 9_____ and
10_____ the essay. I think the professor will be
impressed with how you've improved it.

⌂ Answers

1. portfolio
2. syllabus
3. ten-page essays (or revisions)
4. due
5. rewriting

6. writing center
7. credit
8. participation
9. revisions
10. resubmit

::::: *Notes*

Chapter

Class Discussions

第 三 章

課堂討論

開學第一天

CD1 12

Are you ready? 先來一點新生訓練介紹，了解課程基本面……

Students in American colleges and universities are expected to contribute to class discussions. Even large lecture classes usually have small discussion sections — groups of about fifteen students from the class that meet with teaching assistants to review and discuss class material. To participate effectively in discussions, you will need to listen carefully to your classmates' viewpoints. And when you make a point, you'll want to make it clearly and efficiently.

　　美國大學生都必須參與課堂討論。即使是大班級的演講課通常也會有小組討論——大約十五個學生一組，與助教會談，一起複習、討論上課的材料。為了能充分參與討論，你必須要仔細聆聽同學的見解。而當你要發表意見時，則必須清楚有效率地表達自己。

進入狀況

Discussion Questions 討論問題卷

Eng. 102 — Introduction to American Literature
Questions for Discussion Sections A, B, C and D
Friday, Dec. 16

☐ *I have never let my schooling interfere with my education.* — Mark Twain
☐ *Education consists mainly in what we have unlearned.* — from Twain's
   Notebook, 1898

1. Think about the various scenes in *Tom Sawyer*. How many of the scenes in
   the novel take place at school or on the way to and from school?

2. Some critics have argued that a central theme of *Tom Sawyer* is the tension
   between freedom and civilization, and that this tension is manifested in
   Twain's discussion of education. Do you agree? If so, do you think that
   Twain consciously planned to deal with these themes as he wrote the book?

3. Consider your reading of *Tom Sawyer* and of the other class materials on
   Twain. Which does Twain feel is more important, school-based learning or
   experiential learning? What is your own opinion?

英文 102 —美國文學概論
A 、 B 、 C 和 D 組的討論題目
十二月十六號星期五

☐ 我從不讓到學校上課妨害我的教育。——馬克吐溫
☐ 教育主要在於學習我們沒有學習到的東西。——出自吐溫的筆記本，一八九八年。

1. 想一想《湯姆歷險記》中的眾多場景。小說中，在學校和上、下學途中的場景有多少個？

2. 有些評論家認爲《湯姆歷險記》之中心主題在於自由和文明之間的緊張關係，而這種緊張關係在馬克吐溫對教育的探討中表露無遺。你同意嗎？如果同意，你是否認爲馬克吐溫在寫這本書時，有計劃地刻意去討論這些主題？

3. 仔細想一想你所唸的《湯姆歷險記》以及其他課堂上唸過的馬克吐溫作品。他覺得何者比較重要，以學校爲主的學習還是由經驗得到的學習？你個人的意見爲何？

 討論 I. ○○ CD1 13

📂 Participating in a Discussion Section

Peter and Cindy attend a discussion section for their English class twice a week. The group is led by Brad Cossey, a Teaching Assistant. Today Brad wants to start a discussion about the novel Tom Sawyer and Mark Twain's views on education.

Brad: How is everyone? Have you all been enjoying *Tom Sawyer*?

Peter: You bet. It's a hilarious book. Some of [1]the language is difficult to understand, though.

Brad: Twain's [2]mastery of [3]colloquial English is a fascinating topic, but today I'd like to discuss the views he expresses about education in Tom Sawyer.

Peter: That's easy: Skip school and [4]have a ball!

Brad: Hmm...

Peter: I'm serious. I mean, it's hardly an advertisement for [5]formal education. It's a book about being free and having fun.

Brad: So you think Twain is [6]opposed to formal education?

Peter: I think he's pretty clearly [7]on the side of freedom and independent learning. I mean, he obviously knows that school isn't much fun.

Brad: That's a [8]perceptive point, Peter.

Peter: Mark Twain himself was a self-educated man. And it shows. In my opinion, the smartest and most interesting people [9]tend to be [10]self-taught.

📁　**參與討論**

彼得和辛蒂每星期參加兩次英文課的小組討論。這個小組由助教科西‧布萊德領導。今天布萊德希望討論《湯姆歷險記》這本小說和馬克吐溫的教育觀。

布萊德：大家好嗎？你們《湯姆歷險記》都讀得很開心吧？

彼得　：那還用說。這是一本令人捧腹的書，不過裡面有些用語不好懂。

布萊德：馬克吐溫對英文口語用法的精巧掌握是一個很好的題目，不過今天我想討論的是他在《湯姆歷險記》中所表達對教育的觀點。

彼得　：那很容易：逃學去玩個痛快！

布萊德：嗯……

彼得　：我是說真的。我的意思是，書中幾乎不宣揚正規教育。這是一本關於自由快活、享受歡樂的書。

布萊德：所以你認為馬克吐溫是反對正規教育的？

彼得　：我認為他無疑是自由和獨立學習的擁護者。我的意思是，顯然他知道學校不怎麼好玩

布萊德：那是個頗有見地的看法，彼得。

彼得　：馬克吐溫他自己本身就是個自學者。這點很明顯。依我看來，最聰明、最有趣的人往往都是靠自學。

　○。

1 the language [ˈlæŋgwɪdʒ] *n.*（書中）用語

2 mastery of 對……的精通

3 colloquial [kəˈlokwɪəl] *adj.* 口語的

4 to have a ball 玩得愉快

5 formal education [ˈfɔml͵ɛdʒəˈkeʃən] *n.*正規教育

6 oppose to 反對

7 on the side of 擁護某一方

8 perceptive [pəˈsɛptɪv] *adj.* 有洞察力的

9 tend to be 有……的傾向

10 self-taught [ˈsɛlfˈtɔt] *adj.* 自修的

:::::: *Take a Break*

 II. ◯ ∘   CD1 14

📂 Participating in a Discussion Section (Continued)

Later in the discussion section, Peter and Cindy are considering the following issue: Which is more important, school-based learning or experiential learning?

Cindy: But Peter, experience is [1] <u>no substitute for</u> getting a degree. In this world, if you don't have the [2] <u>credentials,</u> you [3] <u>can't even get in the door.</u>

Peter: I have a different [4] <u>viewpoint.</u> Look at Tom Sawyer. He hardly ever went to school, and look at all of the things that he learned.

Cindy: [5] <u>I see your point,</u> but you need to remember that Tom Sawyer was written over a hundred years ago. Life is different now.

Peter: You mean that life is more competitive now, [6] <u>relative to</u> then?

Cindy: You don't need to take my word for it. Just look at the [7] <u>evidence.</u>

Peter: For example?

Cindy: Answer this question: If you were to get a C in this class, would you be able to get into law school?

Peter: No, probably not.

Cindy: [8] <u>That's my point.</u> To succeed in life, you need a good education.

Peter: Well, I think we have to [9] <u>define</u> success. But before we do, let me ask you a question: Have you ever met an [10] <u>educated idiot</u>?

Cindy: A what?

Peter: Someone who has learned everything they know from books. In reality, they know very little about life and how to live it.

Cindy: Hmm... I guess maybe I do know a few people like that!

繼續參與討論

在稍後的討論中，彼得和辛蒂在思考下述的議題：哪一個比較重要，以學校為主的學習或是由經驗得到的學習？

辛蒂：不過，彼得，經驗並不能取代學歷。在這個世界上，如果你沒有文憑的話，你根本一點機會都沒有。

彼得：我有不同的看法。看看頑童湯姆，他幾乎都沒去上學，而妳瞧他學了那麼多東西。

辛蒂：我了解你的意思，但是你不要忘了《湯姆歷險記》是一百年以前寫的。現在的生活方式已經大不相同了。

彼得：妳是說與當時相比，現在的生活比較競爭嗎？

辛蒂：你不用相信我的話，只要看看證據就夠了。

彼得：譬如說？

辛蒂：回答我這個問題：如果你在這堂課拿了個 C，你有可能進入法學院就讀嗎？

彼得：不，大概不行。

辛蒂：那就是我的重點。生活中要成功，你需要良好的教育。

彼得：嗯，我想我們必須為成功下個定義。不過先讓我問妳一個問題：妳有沒有碰到過受過教育的大白癡？

辛蒂：碰過什麼？

彼得：那種一切知識都是從書本上學來的人。實際上，他們對生活和如何過生活所知甚少。

辛蒂：嗯……我想我的確認識幾個那樣的人。

○。

1. no substitute [ˋsʌbstəˏtjut] for 不能取代

2. the credentials [krɪˋdɛnʃəlz] *n.* 資格證書（此處指文憑）

3. can't even get in the door 連門都進不去

4. viewpoint [ˋvjuˏpɔɪnt] *n.* 觀點

5. I see your point. 我了解你的意思。

6. relative to 與……相對而言

7. evidence [ˋɛvədəns] *n.* 證據

8. That's my point. 那就是我的重點。

9. define [dɪˋfaɪn] *v.* 下定義

10. educated idiot [ˋɛdʒəˏketɪdˋɪdɪət] *n.* 受過教育的白癡

補充單字 In Context CD1 🎧 15

opinion 意見

Classmate: In my **opinion**, Professor Clark is the best lecturer in the history department.

☞ You: I don't have an opinion about Professor Clark. I've never taken one of his classes.

同學：　依我看來，克拉克教授是歷史系中最棒的講師了。

你：　　我對克拉克教授沒特別的看法。我從沒修過他的課。

---

perspective 觀點

☞ You: World War II must have been a difficult time in America.

Professor: Just imagine what it was like from the **perspective** of the Russians.

你：　　美國在二次世界大戰期間一定十分艱苦。

教授：　你可想像從俄國人的觀點來看又會是什麼光景。

prime example 最好的例證

Classmate:　It looks to me like the president is giving the sugar growers a special deal.

TA:　Of course he is. It's a **prime example** of how he abuses his powers.

同學：　看起來總統似乎給糖農特別的待遇。

助教：　當然是囉！這是他濫權最好的例證。

---

misperception 錯誤的認知

Classmate:　The Brazilians in Japan are responsible for a lot of crime.

☞ You:　Are you sure? That might just be a **misperception**. It's easy to blame foreigners for problems.

同學：　在日本的巴西人要為許多犯罪事件負責。

你：　你確定嗎？或許那只是個錯誤的認知。把問題怪罪在外國人身上太方便了。

persuasive 有說服力的

☞ You: After listening to Mr. Klein's speech, I agree that we should all wear uniforms.

Classmate: No doubt about it, he made a very **persuasive** speech.

你： 聽了克萊恩先生的演講之後，我贊同我們應該都要穿制服。

同學： 毫無疑問地，他的演講十分具有說服力。

conclusion 結論

TA: Your **conclusion** really surprises me.

☞ You: You may be surprised, but I think it's correct.

助教： 你的結論叫我十分驚訝。

你： 你或許感到訝異，但是我認為那是正確的。

incorrect 不正確的

Classmate:　I think your conclusion is **incorrect**.

☞ You:　　　You mean you don't believe there's a relationship between poverty and crime?

同學：　　　我認為你的結論不正確。

你：　　　　你的意思是說你不認為貧窮和犯罪之間有所關連？

---

inconclusive 未獲結論的；不能使人信服的

Classmate:　I think I've proved my point.

☞ You:　　　I don't think so. I think your evidence is **inconclusive**.

同學：　　　我想我證明了我的論點。

你：　　　　我可不這麼認為。我認為你的證據不能使人信服。

position 立場；見解

TA:	I think your **position** is very weak.
☞ You:	No, you're wrong. I have a lot of evidence to support my position that there is a relationship between violence and American TV.
助教：	我認為你的論點十分薄弱。
你：	不，你錯了。我有許多證據能支持暴力和美國電視節目有關的這個論點。

dogmatic 獨斷的；武斷的

Classmate:	You don't have to be so **dogmatic**. We are just having a discussion.
☞ You:	Sorry, sometimes I feel very passionate about women's rights.
同學：	你不必這麼武斷。我們只是討論一下。
你：	對不起，有時候談到女權我就會很激動。

留學 Survival Kits CD1 🎧 16

1 號法寶　Logical Fallacies　謬誤推理

不論是在會議室或是在教室裡，如果你想提出強而有力的論點，都要避免謬誤的推理。謬誤的推理是提出似乎具有說服力的論點，然而實際上並不合乎邏輯。以下是四種最常見的典型：

☞ The Appeal to Authority 訴諸於權威

Explanation: Citing an expert to support a point does not prove the point. Just because a professor, doctor, or president says it is true, doesn't make it true. Experts often disagree, and experts have been wrong.

說明：引述專家的話來加以支持一個論點並無法證明該論點。只是因為某個教授、醫生或是總統說那是真的，並不代表那一定是真的。專家常會意見相左，而且專家也會犯錯。

Example: "In the year 2007, the sun is going to explode and the earth will be consumed in a great ball of fire and energy. You don't believe me? Well, read Dr. Gupta's book. He has a PhD in astronomy. He knows!"

例子：「二〇〇七年的時候，太陽將會爆炸，而且地球會被燒毀，成為一顆有巨大能量的火球。你不相信我？好吧，去看古塔博士的書吧。他是天文學的博士。他最懂了。」

☞ **The Post Hoc Fallacy** 事後歸因謬誤

Explanation: Post hoc is a Latin phrase meaning "after this." It's used to describe this kind of false causal argument: "Just because A happened before B, A caused B." Obviously, that's not necessarily true.

說明：Post hoc 是拉丁字，意思是「在此之後」。用來形容下面這種不正確的因果論：「就因為 A 在 B 之前發生，所以是 A 導致了 B 。」顯然，那不一定是真的。

Example: "Before they opened the casino, Neon City was safe. Statistics show that crime has increased since the casino opened. The casino is causing the increase in crime. I even had my purse stolen last week!"

例子：「在他們開設賭場前，霓虹城是很安全的。統計數字顯示自從賭場開了之後，犯罪事件就增加了。是賭場造成犯罪的增加。我上個禮拜皮包甚至被偷了！」

☞ **Attacking the Person 人身攻擊**

Explanation: The person making an argument is attacked rather than the argument itself.

說明：受到抨擊的是提出論點的人，而非該論點。

Example: "You're from Bangladesh and you never went to college! You can't understand economics!"

例子：「你來自於孟加拉，而且從來沒唸過大學！你不可能懂得經濟學！」

☞ **Begging the Question 以未經證實的觀點為立論依據**

Explanation: An argument that does not prove anything but merely restates premises as conclusions.

說明：一個不能證明任何事的論證，只單單重述前提作為結論。

Example: "I already told you, I'm not lying! Therefore, I must be telling the truth!"

例子：「我已經告訴過你了，我沒有說謊！因此，我說的一定是事實！」

2 號 法 寶　Keep It Simple　保持簡單

☞ The simple truth is that if you want to make a good argument, you have to have a good idea. Complicated language and phrases won't help you if your ideas are weak or poorly thought through. When it comes time to speak in class, don't worry if you haven't mastered all the jargon, phrases, and idioms. Just state your ideas as clearly and simply as possible.

☞ 最簡單的道理就是如果你想提出一個好的論證,你就必須要有一個好的見解。如果你的見解很薄弱、貧乏,即使使用複雜的用語和措辭並不會有所幫助。在課堂上要發表意見時,如果你尚末精熟所有的術語、慣用語和成語其實不用擔心,只要盡可能清楚、簡單地表達你的想法就可以了。

:::::: *Quiz*

Complete the dialogue.

Persuasive, position, perceptive, perspective, opinion,
see your point, raised... questions, mastery of

Cindy: You 1_____ some interesting _____ in the discussion section yesterday.

Peter: I just tried to give my 2_____ without worrying what anybody would think.

Cindy: You have nothing to worry about. Your ideas are very 3_____.

Peter: Thanks, Cindy. You have an interesting 4_____, too.

Cindy: But my arguments are not very 5_____.

Peter: Why do you say that?

Cindy: You weren't convinced by them, were you?

Peter: Well, uh, I mean, I could 6_____

Cindy: But I didn't convince you to change your 7_____, did I?

Peter: No, you didn't. I guess your 8_____ of the material was indeed insufficient. Plus, I'm very stubborn.

• •

📁 Answers

1. raised... questions

2. opinion

3. perceptive

4. perspective

5. persuasive

6. see your point

7. position

8. mastery of

Notes

Chapter 4

Talking With Your Professor

第四章

與教授談話

開學第一天　　　　CD1 17

Are you ready? 先來一點新生訓練介紹，了解課程基本面……

During certain hours each week—as noted in the course syllabus—professors make themselves available to meet with individual students. Although you may be a little shy about meeting with your professor, office hours are an excellent opportunity that you shouldn't miss. If you are having problems in class, most professors are happy to offer advice. If you're doing well but want to further explore the class material, most professors are delighted to offer recommendations for further reading. Professors can also recommend other appropriate classes and may even be willing to give you some good career advice.

　　如課程大綱上寫明的，教授在每個星期的特定時段會挪出時間與學生個別會談。雖然跟教授會面你可能會覺得有點害羞，但是這段辦公時間是你絕不能錯過的絕佳機會。如果你在課堂上有問題，大多數的教授會很樂於提供建議。如果你進展得還不錯，不過想更深入探討所學內容，大多數的教授會樂於為你推薦進階書目。教授也會推薦其他適合你的課程，甚至會為你未來的規劃提供一些不錯的建議。

進入狀況

📂 Paper with Corrections 報告作業修改

Prof. Donald King

Eng. 101 Intro to Academic Writing

Tom Sawyer: A Nineteenth-Century Socrates
            Cindy Ho

Cindy, Come to see me during my office hours on Friday afternoon. -D. King

Socrates, the Greek philosopher born in 469 ~~BC~~ and sentenced to death in Athens ~~by drinking hemlock~~ in 399 ~~BC,~~ believed that the most important philosophical question in life is; How should I live my life? In my opinion, it is hard to find the answer to that question in books. You ~~and I and everybody else, too,~~ can only learn how to best live life by living it. When it comes to this most important question, book-learning is no ~~substitution~~ for experience. Take, for example, a person who reads a book about how to drive a car. The book explains the functions of, say, the stearing wheel, breaks and gas pedal. But once on the road, a new driver quickly learns that there is much more to driving then knowing how a car works and the proper method of driving it. ~~This may be a simplistic example that demonstrates, in a very straightforward way,~~ that one needs experience driving to best learn how to drive.

Like Socrates, Mark Twain's character Tom Sawyer...

BCE is now preferred over BC.

Unnecessary: How he died is not important to your thesis.

Use a colon ":" here to replace semicolon.

Delete: Wordy!

substitute

Spelling!

Wrong word!

than

Wordy! Try, "This simple example demonstrates..."

📂 Cindy's Paper 辛蒂的作業

唐諾德・金 教授
英文 101 初級學術寫作

頑童湯姆：十九世紀的蘇格拉底

何辛蒂

　　出生於西元前 469 年，而於西元前 399 年在雅典被處以服毒芹而死的希臘哲學家蘇格拉底相信，生命中最重要的哲學問題是：我該過怎樣的人生？我認為，這個問題很難從書本中找到答案。你和我和所有的人都一樣，只能從生活中學習怎麼活得精彩。當談論到這個重要的問題時，書本的知識是無法替代經驗的。舉個例子來說，有個人讀了一本教人開車的書。這本書中解釋了一些功能，例如如何操作方向盤、煞車和油門。但是一旦上了路，一個新手駕駛將很快就會發現，除了知道車子如何運轉以及正確的駕駛方式之外，真正要學的東西可多得多了。這或許是個很簡單的例子，用很直接的方式說明了有駕駛經驗才能讓人學好開車。

　　就像蘇格拉底一樣，馬克吐溫筆下的人物湯姆・索爾……

討論 I. ○。

CD1 18

📂 Professor's Office Hours

Cindy goes to see Professor King during his office hours to discuss her paper.

Cindy: Thanks for meeting with me, Professor King. I wanted to talk to you about my paper. I got a C, but I think I can do better. I'd like to get some advice and then rewrite it.

King: I'll be happy to help. That's why I asked you to come in. Revision is the most important part of the writing process. Your first [1] draft is never your best.

Cindy: Can you show me where I went wrong?

King: You have an interesting [2] thesis — that book learning is no substitute for real life experience. And your discussion of Tom Sawyer and Socrates is lively and very [3] original.

Cindy: Sounds like I should have got an A.

King: The problem is that your paper lacks [4] focus. You try to do too much. There are seven paragraphs here where you [5] relate almost the entire life story of Socrates.

Cindy: I see your point. Socrates is a good example for me to use, but my essay really should be about the novel. I could [6] cut out a lot of that.

King: Right. You have an interesting idea to work with. Focus on it. Cut out anything that doesn't support your thesis. Not just [7] extraneous ideas, but also any extra words. [8] Tighten everything up. If you [9] put some work into this, it'll be a good paper. I'd like you to stop by the Writing Center sometime this week and talk to someone there about your paper.

Cindy: Thanks. I'll do that.

在教授的辦公時間去找教授

辛蒂在金教授的辦公時間去找他討論她的報告。

辛蒂：金教授，謝謝你跟我見面。我想跟你討論我的報告。我得了個
　　　C，可是我認為我可以做得更好。我想聽聽您的建議，然後重寫
　　　一次。

金　：我很樂意幫忙。那也是我叫妳來的原因。修改是寫作過程中最重
　　　要的一個部分。第一次的草稿絕對不會是最好的成品。

辛蒂：你可以告訴我我哪裡出錯了嗎？

金　：妳的論點很有意思 —— 書本上的知識無法取代實際生活經驗。而
　　　且妳對湯姆・索爾和蘇格拉底所作的討論很生動，也很有創意。

辛蒂：聽起來我應該拿 A 的。

金　：問題在於妳的報告缺少重心。妳想寫的太廣泛了。妳用了七個段
　　　落，幾乎把蘇格拉底一生的故事都說完了。

辛蒂：我了解你的意思了。我用蘇格拉底作例子很好，但是事實上我的
　　　報告應該是關於這本小說才對。我可以把那部分的東西刪掉一大
　　　半。

金　：沒錯。妳的想法很有意思，但是寫作時要把重點擺在那上面。刪
　　　除那些無法支持妳的論點的部份 —— 不只是無關的概念，還有多
　　　餘的用字。要簡潔有力。如果妳在這方面多用點心，這將會是一
　　　篇好報告。我希望妳這個禮拜能找個時間去寫作教室，找個人談
　　　談妳的報告。

辛蒂：謝謝。我會的。

1 draft [dræft] *n.* 草稿

2 thesis [ˋθisɪs] *n.* 論點

3 original [əˋrɪdʒənl] *adj.* 具獨創性的

4 focus [ˋfokəs] *n.* 焦點

5 relate [rɪˋlet] *v.* 敘述，說（事）

6 cut (out) 刪掉

7 extraneous [ɪkˋstrenɪəs] *adj.* 無關的

8 Tighten everything up. 要簡潔有力。

9 put some work into sth. 在某事上用心

::::: *Take a Break*

 II. ○ ○

CD1 19

📁 Visiting the Writing Center

Cindy visits the Writing Center to get some help with her paper.

Cindy: Hi, my name is Cindy Ho. I have this paper ...

Ken: ... that you'd like someone to look at? Nice to meet you, Cindy. I'm Ken Douglas. What can I help you with?

Cindy: This essay. It's for English101. I want it to be more focused and [1] <u>concise</u>.

Ken: Hey, you know what you want. That's a good start. Let me take a look.

Cindy: Thanks a lot. I really appreciate it.

Ken: *Tom Sawyer*! I love that book! OK, I'm going to use some [2] <u>editing symbols</u> to show you where I think you might make changes. Hmm ... Like here, where you'd be better off using the [3] <u>active voice</u> rather than the passive.

Cindy: Great ... Hey! Why are you [4] <u>crossing that out</u>?

Ken: I think you can [5] <u>delete</u> this entire sentence. It's [6] <u>redundant</u>.

Cindy: Oh, I guess you're right. And I see you found another [7] <u>trouble spot</u>. I didn't know how to make that [8] <u>transition</u>.

Ken: Transitions can be tough. Sometimes you just have to keep thinking and [9] <u>working on it</u> until you find a solution. Writing really is hard work. Let me see if I can help you [10] <u>come up with</u> a good transition.

Cindy: This is really great, Ken. Thank you so much. I can't believe this is free!

造訪寫作教室

辛蒂到寫作教室去尋求協助以改善她的報告。

辛蒂：嗨，我叫何辛蒂。我有一篇報告……

肯　：……需要有人幫妳看一下？很高興認識妳，辛蒂。我叫肯・道格拉斯。有什麼我可以幫妳的嗎？

辛蒂：這篇報告。這是英文 101 的作業。我想讓它更有重點、更簡潔。

肯　：嘿，妳知道自己要什麼。那是個好的開始。讓我看一下。

辛蒂：多謝你了。我真的很感激。

肯　：湯姆歷險記！我很喜歡那本書！好，我要用一些編輯符號來標示我認為妳可能得修改的地方。嗯……像這裡，妳最好用主動語態，不要用被動。

辛蒂：好極了……嘿! 你為什麼把那個劃掉？

肯　：我認為妳可以把這整個句子刪掉。它是多餘的。

辛蒂：噢，我想你是對的。我看到你還發現了另一個有問題的地方。我不曉得那個地方該怎麼讓語氣轉折。

肯　：啓承轉折並不容易。有時候妳得不斷思考、咀嚼才能找到解決的方法。寫作的確很辛苦。讓我看看能不能幫妳想出一個好的轉折語。

辛蒂：肯，這真是太棒了。非常謝謝你。我不敢相信這是免費的！

。

1. concise [kən`saɪs] *adj.* 簡潔的

2. editing symbol [`ɛdɪtɪŋ ˌsɪmbl̩] *n.* 編輯符號

3. active voice [`æktɪv `vɔɪs] *n.* 主動語態

4. cross sth. out 將某物（畫線）刪掉

5. delete [dɪ`lit] *v.* 刪掉

6. redundant [rɪ`dʌndənt] *adj.* 多餘的；（措辭）冗長的

7. trouble spot [`trʌbl̩ ˌspɑt] *n.* 有問題之處

8. transition [træn`zɪʃən] *n.* 過渡；轉折

9. working on it〔口語〕在某事上作努力

10. come up with sth.〔口語〕想到（主意）；找出（解答）

●●●補充單字 In Context CD1 🎧 20

semicolon / punctuation 分號／標點符號

Ken:	Do you understand when to use a **semi-colon**?
☞ You:	Yeah, but I try to avoid fancy **punctuation** when I write.

肯： 你了解什麼時候得用分號嗎？

你： 知道，不過我寫作時會試著避免用裝飾性的標點符號。

---

verbose 冗長的

☞ You:	When he said my paper was too **verbose**, did he mean it was too long?
TA:	No, he meant that you should eliminate unnecessary words. Try to say things as simply as possible.

你： 當他說我的報告太冗長，他的意思是我寫太長了嗎？

助教： 不，他的意思是你應該刪掉不必要的字。試著盡可能用簡單的方式來表達。

jargon 專業名詞

☞ You:　　　　How did you like my essay?

　Classmate:　I can't understand all the technical terms. It would be much better if you eliminated all the **jargon**.

　你：　　　你覺得我的文章如何？

　同學：　　我完全不懂那些科技名詞。如果你能把那些專業名詞都刪掉的話會好得多。

---

theme 主題

　Classmate:　I'm not really sure what the main **theme** of my paper should be.

☞ You:　　　　I know. That's your problem. You don't know what you want to write about.

　同學：　　我不太確定我報告的主題應該是什麼。

　你：　　　我知道。那正是你的問題。你不知道你想寫些什麼。

writing style 寫作風格

☞ You: Did you like Omar's paper?

Classmate: It's OK. I mean, it's well done. It's just that his **writing style** is so dull.

你： 你覺得奧瑪的報告怎麼樣？

同學： 還可以。我的意思是，他寫得不錯，只是他的寫作風格太無趣了。

---

brainstorm 腦力激盪

☞ You: What did Professor King mean when he said that we should do some **brainstorming** this weekend?

TA: We're supposed to think about what we want to write about and just write down whatever we think of.

你： 金教授說我們這個週末要做點腦力激盪，是什麼意思？

助教： 我們應該要思考一下我們想寫的東西，並寫下任何我們想到的。

outline / organize 大綱／組織

☞ You: Do you find it helpful to make an **outline** before you start working on a paper?

Classmate: Absolutely. It's a great way to **organize** your ideas—and to make sure that you have some decent ideas, before you start writing.

你： 你覺得在著手寫報告前先擬一份大綱有幫助嗎？

同學： 當然有。那是幫助你把概念組織起來的好方法 —— 而且可以確保在你開始寫作之前，已經有了一些相當好的想法。

to go over 仔細檢查

Classmate: You should **go over** this one more time. It still needs a little work.

☞ You: Again? How many times do I have to write this same paper?

同學： 你應該把這篇文章再仔細看過一次。它還有一些些要加強的地方。

你： 還要再一次？同一篇報告我要寫多少遍呀？

to get sick of sth. / to hang in there 對……厭倦／堅持下去

☞ You: I'm really **getting sick of** working on this paper.

Classmate: **Hang in there.** You'll be done soon.

你： 我真的對處理這份報告感到越來越厭倦了。

同學： 要堅持下去。你很快就會完成的。

---

to take a look / to turn it in 看一看／繳交

☞ You: I think I'm finally done. Will you help me proofread this?

Classmate: I'll be glad to **take a look**. When do you need to **turn it in**?

你： 我想我終於完成了。你可以幫我校對嗎？

同學： 我很樂意看一看。你什麼時候得交出去呢？

留學 Survival Kits CD1  21

1 號法寶 **Tips for talking with professors**
可以用來跟教授開啓話題的語句

☞ **Asking for advice 請求建議**

• "Hello, Professor Smith. I've selected a topic for my final paper, and I wanted to discuss it with you."

• "Hi, Professor Howell. I'm having trouble finding enough resources for my mid-term project, and I was hoping you could give me some advice."

• "How's it going, Professor? I'm trying to choose between two history classes for next semester and I'd like to ask for your advice."

☞ **Asking for help 請求幫助**

• "How are you, Professor Newton? I'm afraid I didn't really understand what you were saying in yesterday's lecture about differential equations. Could I ask you a few questions about them?"

• "Hi, Professor. I'm Lenny. I'm a student in your World War II class. I'm really interested in the siege of Stalingrad and was wondering if you might recommend some books."

☞ **Asking for an extension** 請求延期

- "Good morning, Professor Scholes. I hate to ask, but I'm swamped with work right now and I was wondering if I could get an extension on my paper. I'll be able to turn in a much better essay if I can have a couple of extra days."

- "Professor Scholes? I was wondering if I could have an extension. I have some personal issues that I have to deal with and I won't have enough time to finish my paper."

☞ **Asking for a grade change** 請求更改成績

- "Professor Van Nistelroy? I think you may have made a mistake when you corrected my exam. Can I show it to you?"

- "Professor Van Nistelroy? I'd like you to have another look at my paper. I worked very hard on it and I think it deserves a better grade than the one I got."

2 號 法 寶 Dealing With Uncooperative Professors
與不配合的教授交涉

☞ Every now and then, you will encounter a professor who does not keep his or her office hours. And professors, like everybody else, can sometimes be grumpy and unpleasant. If you are unlucky enough to have a professor like this, don't be intimidated. Professors are paid to do a job and part of their job is to teach. If they haven't explained something clearly, you have every right to ask them for further assistance.

☞ 有時你會碰到不遵守辦公時間的教授。而教授就跟一般人一樣,有時會脾氣暴躁,令人覺得不愉快。如果你運氣不好遇到這樣子的教授,不用怕。教授是受聘來工作的,而教學是他們工作的一部份。如果他們沒有清楚地將事情說明清楚,你有充分的權力要求他們作進一步的協助。

:::::: *Quiz*

Complete the dialogue.

concise, draft, editing symbols, themes, tighten everything up, thesis, focus, crossed out, writing center, trouble spots, cut

Cindy: Look at this 1_____ of my English paper.

Peter: Somebody made a bunch of marks on your paper. Whose writing is this?

Cindy: I went to the 2_____ for help. A guy named Ken helped me. Those are his 3_____.

Peter: He liked your 4_____.

Cindy: He said that overall it is a good paper. But there are lots of 5_____.

Peter: Like here. He's 6_____ this whole paragraph. I guess he wants you to 7_____ it.

Cindy: Yes. He says I should try to be more 8_____ and 9_____ more on the main 10_____ of my paper.

Peter: Basically, it looks he has recommended that you 11_____. That's pretty good advice, I guess.

. . . .

📁 Answers

1. draft

2. writing center

3. editing symbols

4. thesis

5. trouble spots

6. crossed out

7. cut

8. concise

9. focus

10. themes

11. tighten everything up

Chapter 5

Taking Notes

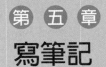

寫筆記

開學第一天

Are you ready? 先來一點新生訓練介紹，了解課程基本面……

Note taking may seem like the dullest of all academic skills, but it is key to your success. It may be difficult at first to understand everything your teacher is saying, but you'll probably be able to catch at least some of the main points. Keeping good notes will help you focus your attention during lectures. Revising and reviewing your notes after class will help you clarify and identify the main points. With a bit of practice, you'll soon be a master note taker.

做筆記似乎是所有做學問的技巧中最無趣的一種，但它可是你成功的關鍵呢！一開始或許會不容易聽懂老師說的每樣東西，不過你可能至少會抓到一些重點。做好筆記能幫助你在上課時集中注意力。課後重新整理、複習筆記能幫助你澄清並確認重點。只要稍加練習，你就會成為做筆記的高手了。

進入狀況

📂 Cindy's Notes 辛蒂的筆記

⊙ Tries to write everything down (and, of course, can't).
　想把每件事都寫下來（當然，是不可能的）。

⊙ Words and ideas written randomly
　字與想法寫得凌亂

⊙ Pretty horsey!
　漂亮的馬兒！

📁 Peter's Notes 彼得的筆記

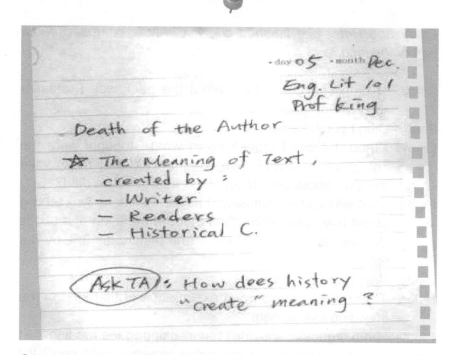

⊙ Notes class, professor, and date.
記下課程名稱、教授名字，與日期

⊙ Only writes clearly organized key points, not complete sentences
只清楚地寫下有組織的重點，非完整的句子

⊙ Writes questions about things he's unsure of
將他不確定的事寫成問題

⊙ Uses symbols: ✪ = key point, Ask TA = question for the teaching assistant
使用符號：✪ = 重點，Ask TA ＝要問助教的問題

 討論 I. ○○。

 CD2 02

📂 Strategies for Taking Notes

Cindy and Peter just finished class. Cindy is confused about part of the lecture.

Cindy: [1] <u>I didn't get that</u> *at all*. What the heck was Professor King talking about?

Peter: Didn't you take notes?

Cindy: I tried. I mean I [2] <u>jotted down</u> what I thought were the [3] <u>main points</u>, but I [4] <u>have no idea</u> what they mean. Like this part about the "death of the author." Who died?

Peter: That was a little confusing, I agree. I think he was talking about how some critics feel that the meaning of a text is created as much by readers and history, as it is by the writer.

Cindy: Was that in the lecture?

Peter: There was a pretty good explanation of that idea in the [5] <u>reading assignment</u>.

Cindy: Hmm. I guess I shouldn't have [6] <u>skipped</u> the reading.

Peter: Why don't we revise our notes together right now? It'll help us understand the lecture better.

Cindy: You want to take notes on your notes?

Peter: In a way, yes. I like to read through my notes while the lecture is still [7] <u>fresh in my mind</u>. Sometimes I make an [8] <u>outline</u> of the main points, or rewrite an idea [9] <u>in my own words</u>. It makes reviewing later much easier. Sometimes I [10] <u>flag something</u> I want to ask Professor King about during his office hours.

Cindy: Hmm... OK. I never knew note taking was so complicated!

📁 作筆記的技巧

彼得與辛蒂剛上完課。辛蒂對於部分的上課內容感到困惑。

辛蒂：我「一點」都不懂。金教授到底在講些什麼？

彼得：妳沒有做筆記嗎？

辛蒂：我試過。我的意思是我匆匆記下了我認為的重點，可是我完全不知道那是什麼意思。譬如像這個「作家之死」的部份，是誰死了呢？

彼得：我同意，那點是有些令人困惑。我想他談的是，有些評論家覺得賦予文意意涵的不只是作者本人，讀者和歷史亦有一番詮釋。

辛蒂：上課時有講到那個嗎？

彼得：在指定閱讀部份中對那個概念有很清楚的解釋。

辛蒂：嗯。我想我不應該略過指定閱讀的。

彼得：咱們現在何不一起重新整理我們的筆記呢？這將有助於我們更加了解上課的內容。

辛蒂：你想用你的筆記再做一次筆記？

彼得：就某方面來說，是的。我喜歡趁上課內容在我腦海中還記憶猶新的時候，把筆記從頭到尾看一次。有時我會把重點寫成大綱，或是把某個概念用我自己的話再寫一次，之後複習起來會容易得多。有時我會把要在金教授辦公時間問他的東西貼上標籤紙。

辛蒂：嗯……好吧。我從來不知道做筆記是這麼地複雜。

1 **I didn't get that.** 那點我不明白。

2 **jot down** 匆匆記下

3 **main points** 重點

4 **have no idea** 不知道

5 **reading assignment** [ˋridɪŋ əˋsaɪnmənt] *n.* 指定閱讀

6 **skipped** [skɪpt] *v.* 略過

7 **fresh in my mind** 記憶猶新

8 **outline** [ˋaʊtˏlaɪn] *n.* 大綱

9 **in my own words** 用我自己的話

10 **to flag sth.** 貼標籤

::::::: *Take a Break*

 ○。 CD2 03

📂 Emailing a Professor

Cindy writes an email to her professor to clear up a few points from the last lecture.

From: cindy.ho@univ.edu
To: d.king@ eng.univ.edu
RE: death of the author

Dear Professor King:

I've been enjoying your class, English 101, and find it very interesting. Recently, I've also found it to be a bit confusing. [1] In particular, I have some questions about last Thursday's lecture on the death of the author.

You don't mean that anybody has really died, do you? [2] According to my friend, Peter, [3] the point is that [4] it doesn't matter what the author has written. Readers create their own meanings when they read. While [5] reviewing my notes, I see that you said: "Historical factors can overwhelm a writer's [6] intended meanings."

Are you trying to say that a writer's [7] intentions don't matter at all? That can't be right, can it? I mean, if there were no writers there would be no books and we wouldn't even be having this conversation. I'm just a little confused about why you said the author has died. [8] I'd appreciate it if you could [9] clarify your meaning. Thank you.

Regards,
Cindy Ho

📁 寫 e-mail 給教授

辛蒂寫 email 給她的教授，想搞清楚上堂課裡的一些觀點。

親愛的金教授：

我一直都很喜歡您的課，英語 101 ，而且我覺得上課很有趣。不過最近我也感到有點困惑。特別是對於上星期四關於作家之死的那堂課，我有一些不明白的地方。

您並非指真的有人死掉，對不對？據我的朋友彼得說，要點在於作者寫些什麼並不重要，讀者在閱讀的時候會有自己的詮譯。我在複習筆記的時候看到您說「歷史因素會顛覆作者原本要傳達的意思」。

您是想說明作家的意念一點也不重要嗎？不應該是這樣的，不是嗎？我的意思是，如果沒有作家，就不會有書，而我們甚至也不會有這段對談了。我只是有點困惑為什麼您說作家已經死了。如果您能將您的意思說明白些，我會十分感激的。謝謝您。

何辛蒂　敬上

必備字彙 ○。

❶ in particular 特別是

❷ According to... 根據……

❸ the point is... 重點是……

❹ it doesn't matter 沒有關係

❺ review [rɪ`vju] n.複習

❻ intended [ɪn`tɛndɪd] adj. 打算中的；有企圖的

❼ intention [ɪn`tɛnʃən] n. 意向

❽ I'd appreciate it. 我會感激。

❾ clarify [`klærə,faɪ] v. 澄清

●●●補充單字 In Context CD2 ♪ 04

assignment 指定作業

Classmate:	Uh-oh. I forgot to write down the **assignment** in my notes.
☞ You:	Don't worry. I wrote it down.
同學：	喔噢，我忘了把作業記在筆記裡。
你：	別擔心。我記下來了。

---

whiteboard 白板

☞ You:	I wish Professor King would write the important ideas from the lecture on the **whiteboard**.
Classmate:	I agree. Sometimes he talks so fast that it is hard to keep up.
你：	我希望金教授能把課堂上重要的概念寫在黑板上。
同學：	我贊成。他有時候講得太快了，很難跟得上。

---

abbreviations 縮寫

TA:	I can't understand your notes. Is this English?
☞ You:	I use a lot of **abbreviations** to save time.
助教：	我看不懂你的筆記。這是英文嗎？
你：	我用了很多的縮寫來節省時間。

legible （字跡）可以辨認的

☞ You:　　　　　Actually, you're right. Some of this is hard to read.

　　TA:　　　　　Taking all those notes won't do you any good if they're not **legible**.

　　你：　　　　　事實上，你是對的。有一些是很難看懂。

　　助教：　　　　如果這些字跡難以辨識的話，做這些筆記就對你沒有任何幫助了。

---

emphasize 強調

　　TA:　　　　　What does this big star mean?

☞ You:　　　　　That the professor **emphasized** this point.

　　助教：　　　　這顆大星星是什麼意思？

　　你：　　　　　那是指教授強調的重點。

example 例子

☞ You: If the professor gives an **example**, I make sure I jot it down.

Classmate: I agree. Examples make things a lot easier to understand.

你： 如果教授有舉例子，我一定會記下來。

同學： 我贊同。舉例子能讓事情更容易瞭解。

---

repeat 重複

Classmate: I like the way Professor King **repeats** the important points.

☞ You: I'm glad he does. Otherwise, I'd never be able to keep up.

同學： 我喜歡金教授重複重點的方式。

你： 我很高興他那樣做。否則我可能跟不上。

elaborate 詳細說明

☞ **You:** Would you **elaborate** a little more on why you think Mark Twain is America's greatest writer?

TA: Don't get me started! I could talk about Mark Twain forever.

你： 你可不可以說詳細一點為什麼你認為馬克吐溫是美國最偉大的作家？

助教： 別讓我打開話匣子！談起馬克吐溫，我可是停不下來的。

---

highlight 強調

☞ **You:** Hey, that's a good idea.

Classmate: Yeah, I switch to my red pen when I want to **highlight** an important point.

你： 嘿，那是個好主意。

同學： 是呀，我想強調某個重點的時候就會換成紅筆。

留學 Survival Kits　CD2 🎧 05

1 號 法 寶　**Note-Taking services** 筆記服務

☞ At some universities, you may be able to purchase notes for some of your classes from a professional note-taking service. Studying someone else's notes is better than not studying at all, but it is not nearly as effective as taking your own notes. It's not just reading notes that helps you learn, but also writing notes. When you attend a lecture and take notes, you are learning how to discriminate between what is important and what is not. This is a very important skill. When you attend a lecture and take notes, your mind is forced into action. The questions and ideas that come to you while taking notes are important to your learning process. Remember, you can never truly learn something until you make it your own.

☞ 在一些大學裡，你也許可以從專業筆記服務社購買到上課用筆記。
讀別人的筆記總是比根本不唸書來得好，不過那遠不及自己做筆記
來得有用。幫助你學習的不僅僅是讀筆記而已，還要親自做筆記。
上課做筆記的時候，你同時是在學習區分什麼是重要、什麼是不重
要的。這是很重要的技巧。上課做筆記時，你的腦筋不得不運轉。
做筆記時想到的問題和概念對你的學習過程很重要。記住，你永遠
無法真正地學會一件事，除非你將它變成自己的東西

2 號 法 寶　6 Tips for effective note taking
有效做筆記的六妙招

1. Be prepared. Complete the required reading and review your notes from the previous lecture. Look over the syllabus to see if there is an outline for the lecture.

2. Find a seat near the front of class to avoid distractions. Listen carefully!

3. Pay attention to words like "First," "Next," "Therefore," "Finally," and "Another important," that signal that the lecturer is about to say something important.

4. Use your own words to summarize the lecturer's main points. Do not try to copy down everything he or she says.

5. Revise and review your notes as soon as possible after the lecture. Your memory will be fresh and this second look will help you remember and learn even more.

6. Use one notebook for each class. Date your notes and give them subject headings.

1. 做好準備。唸完指定的閱讀並複習前堂課的筆記。查閱課程大綱，看看有沒有該堂課的綱要。

2. 找靠近前面的位置坐以避免分心。注意聽講！

3. 留心像是「首先」、「接下來」、「因此」、「最後」、「另一個重要的」等字眼，因為這些字眼意味授課者將要談到的是重要的東西。

4. 用你自己的話來摘要授課者所說的重點。不要嘗試抄下他或她講的每一個字。

5. 上完課後盡快重新整理並且複習你的筆記，因為你的記憶猶新，而且再看一次能幫助你記得更多、學得更多。

6. 每一門課用一本筆記本。在你的筆記上註明日期和科目標題。

3 號 法 寶　Taking notes while you read
閱讀時的筆記

☞ You can also put your note-taking skills to good use when you read. Taking notes while you read can help focus your attention and increase your retention the same way it does when you listen to a lecture. It's easy to become a passive reader and just skim over the words. But if you have your pen in hand and use it to jot down a note or a question mark or to rewrite an idea in your own words, you'll be sure to absorb the meaning of what you are reading.

☞ 在閱讀的時候你也可以妥善利用做筆記的技巧。在閱讀的時候做筆記可以幫助你集中注意力並提昇你的記憶力，就跟你在聽課時一樣。做一個被動的讀者，光是瀏覽一下文字是很容易的。不過如果你手中有筆，並用它來記個筆記，或是畫個問號，或是用你自己的話把某個概念重寫一次，你一定吸收將所讀內容的意涵。

4 號法寶 **Signal Phrases** 結論

There are a number of phrases that should alert you to the fact that something important is coming up during a lecture. Good speakers commonly use these phrases to make things easy for listeners. Consider the following list of examples:

在上課時，有不少語句可以提醒你重點即將出現。好的授課者通常會使用這些語句以便利聽課的人。注意以下列出的例子：

☞ 結論

- "Therefore ..."
- "In conclusion ..."
- "As a result ..."
- "Finally ..."
- "In summary ...""

☞ 提醒重點

- "Now this is important ..."
- "Remember that ..."
- "The important idea is that ..."
- "The basic concept here is ..."

☞ 條列重點

- "There are three reasons why ..."
- "First, ... Second, ... Third, ..."
- "And most important, ..."

☞ 舉例證

- "On the other hand ..."
- "For example ..."
- "On the contrary ..."
- "Similarly ..."
- "Also ..."
- "Furthermore ..."
- "As an example ..."
- "For instance ..."

::::: *Quiz*

Complete the dialogue.

flag, reviewed, in summary, didn't get, reading assignment, to jot down, main points, fresh in your mind

Peter: Is this it? Where are the rest of your notes?

Cindy: I'm sorry, Peter. I was going to follow your note-taking advice.

Peter: OK, right. You 1_____ the 2_____ before class?

Cindy: Yes. That's where my trouble started. I 3_____ the article, so I was up late trying to understand it.

Peter: OK, but your notes... you were supposed 4_____ the 5_____.

Cindy: And I was going to 6_____ the really key ideas with red stars.

Peter: What happened?

Cindy: I was so sleepy, I just couldn't concentrate. So I just waited until I heard him say, "7_____," and then I wrote down what he said next.

Peter: Well, I guess you can review that while it's still 8_____. Shouldn't be too taxing.

· ·

📁 Answers

1. reviewed

2. reading assignment

3. didn't get

4. to jot down

5. main points

6. flag

7. in summary

8. fresh in your mind

Notes

開學第一天

CD2 06

Are you ready? 先來一點新生訓練介紹，了解課程基本面……

Students are often required to work on group presentations. One reason that teachers like to assign group presentation is that they hope to teach their students how to cooperate effectively with their classmates.Typically, only a single grade, which represents the group's performance as a whole, is given for presentations. To create an effective presentation, students must evaluate the strengths and weaknesses of each group member and try to distribute the work so that each member's strengths are utilized.

學生通常會被要求要做分組報告。老師們喜歡指派學生做分組報告的原因之一是，他們希望教導學生如何有效率地與同學合作。一般來說，分組報告只會有一個成績，代表整組全體的表現。要做好一個報告，學生們必須評估每一個組員的長處和弱點，然後分配工作，以便充分運用各個成員的長處。

進入狀況

📁 Group Presentation Assignment and Guidelines 分組報告作業及指南

Pol-Sci 103 International relations
Prof. Jon Hardt

Assignment:

Together with two classmates, prepare a fifteen-minute presentation on one aspect of immigration. Groups may focus on how different countries approach a single issue, such as work permits or language policy, or they may focus on several different issues in a single country.

Guidelines for successful group presentations:

1. Divide the work evenly among group members.
2. Narrow your topic (don't try to cover more than is realistic).
3. Adequate research is critical to success. Be certain that the information you present is complete and accurate.
4. Your presentation should be unified and carefully organized. Ensure that it is not several separate mini-presentations.
5. Each group member should participate equally during the presentation.
6. Have a dress rehearsal to practice your presentation.

政治學 103 —國際關係概論
強・哈德特教授

作業

與兩位同學合作，針對移民的某一面向做十五分鐘的報告。各小組可以著重於討論不同國家如何處理某一項議題，例如工作許可證或是語言政策，或者著重在討論單一國家中不同的議題。

分組報告成功指南

1. 組員將工作平均分配。
2. 將題目的範圍縮小（不要試圖含蓋超出能力可及的範圍）。
3. 充分的研究是成功的關鍵。要確定你們發表的資訊是完整而且是正確的。
4. 你們的報告應該有整體性並且有嚴密的結構。要確保不會變成幾個不同的小報告。
5. 在上台報告的時候每個組員都應該平均參與。
6. 上台發表之前要先彩排練習。

＊注意：套色部分為以下討論 I.、II.對話內重複使用的字彙，並加上了音標註解。

 ○ ◦

CD2 🎧 07

📁 Preparing for a Presentation

Cindy, Peter and Darren are meeting for coffee after class and discussing the presentation they've been assigned to give.

Cindy: We're supposed to give a ¹ <u>presentation</u> about ² <u>immigration</u>? I don't know anything about immigration.

Peter: We'll have to do some ³ <u>research</u>, Cindy.

Darren: First of all, we need to ⁴ <u>narrow our focus</u>.

Cindy: Yeah, immigration ⁵ <u>in general</u> is way too ⁶ <u>broad</u>.

Peter: I agree. Why don't we focus on Japan? Immigration is a serious ⁷ <u>issue</u> there. I lived in Yokohama two summers ago, so I know a little about it.

Darren: And remember in our lecture, Professor Hardt briefly mentioned the Brazilian immigrant community in Japan?

Cindy: I've heard that the Japanese aren't very welcoming, but that they need immigrants. Their population is declining.

Peter: Is that really true? Anyway, I think it'll be an interesting ⁸ <u>project</u> to work on.

Cindy: So it's ⁹ <u>settled</u>: "Immigration in Modern Japan."

Darren: Sounds good. Why don't we meet again tomorrow before class to ¹⁰ <u>make a plan</u>.

🗁 準備報告

辛蒂、彼得和德倫下課後碰面喝咖啡，並討論他們要做的分組報告
作業。

辛蒂：我們得做一個關於移民問題的報告？對於移民我一無所知。

彼得：我們必須先做點研究，辛蒂。

德倫：首先，我們要把題目範圍縮小。

辛蒂：是呀，討論一般的移民問題，範圍太廣泛了。

彼得：我同意。我們何不把重點放在日本呢？移民在那裡是一個嚴重的
　　　問題。我兩年前的夏天在橫濱住過，所以我略知一二。

德倫：而且你們記得上課時哈德特教授曾簡短地提到日本的巴西移民社
　　　會嗎？

辛蒂：我聽說日本人並沒有抱持很歡迎的態度，但是他們需要移民。他
　　　們的人口在下降中。

彼得：那是真的嗎？不論怎麼說，我想這個研究做起來會很有意思。

辛蒂：那就這麼定案了："現代日本的移民"

德倫：聽起來不錯。我們明天上課之前何不再碰個面，把計畫擬好。

○。

① presentation [ˌprɛznˋteʃən] *n.* 發表；（口頭）報告

② immigration [ˌɪməˋgreʃən] *n.* 移民（指自外移入）

③ research [rɪˋsɝtʃ] *n.* 研究

④ narrow our focus 縮小重點範圍

⑤ in general 一般的；一般來說

⑥ broad [brɔd] *adj.* 廣泛

⑦ issue [ˋɪʃʊ] *n.* 議題

⑧ project [ˋprɑdʒɛkt] *n.* 計畫

⑨ settled [ˋsɛtḷd] *v.* 決定；解決

⑩ make a plan 擬計畫

::::: *Take a Break*

 討論 II. ○○

📁 Dividing up the Work

The next morning, Cindy, Peter and Darren continue their conversation.

Darren: Okay, now that we've selected our topic, we need to figure out an appropriate [1] division of labor.

Peter: I like working in the library. I wouldn't mind doing most of the research. Actually, I already [2] stopped by the [3] reference library last night and found some [4] relevant data.

Cindy: Whoa! A real [5] go-getter! I'm glad you're on our team, Peter.

Darren: If you guys want, I could assemble the [6] materials into a speech. I'm a pretty good writer and I'm not too bad at [7] public speaking.

Peter: The only problem is, I think we should all participate in the presentation. Otherwise it'll look like you did all the work. Why don't you do the writing and then help coach Cindy and I on our delivery. We can take turns talking during the presentation.

Darren: That's fine with me.

Cindy: I've had some classes in [8] graphic design. I could put together a good PowerPoint slide show with graphs and charts. And we could even use some photographs to show the human side of the issue.

Peter: That's a great idea, Cindy. That way our presentation won't be too dry or dull.

Cindy: Thanks. If you work on the hard data, Peter, I can [9] track down some good photographs that'll help tell our story.

Darren: Good work, team. Let's meet every Wednesday and Sunday to [10] update each other on our progress.

📂 分配工作

隔天早上，辛蒂、彼得和德倫繼續他們的談話。

德倫：好，既然我們已經選好了我們的題目，我們得想想如何分配好工作。

彼得：我喜歡待在圖書館蒐集資料，我不介意做大部分的研究工作。事實上，我昨晚已經去過了參考資料室，並且找到了一些相關的資訊。

辛蒂：哇！真是幹勁十足！我真高興你跟我們一組，彼得。

德倫：如果你們要的話，我可以把資料彙整成講稿。我的寫作能力挺好的，而且我在公開演說方面也不差。

彼得：唯一的問題是，我認為我們全都應該上台報告。要不然看起來會像是你一手包辦全部的工作。何不由你來撰稿，然後協助指導辛蒂和我做發表呢？我們在報告時可以輪流講。

德倫：這我沒問題。

辛蒂：我修過一些平面設計的課。我可以用圖表做出一個很棒的簡報投影片。而且我們可以用一些照片來表現出這個議題比較人性化的部份。

彼得：這是個很棒的主意，辛蒂。這樣一來我們的報告就不會太枯燥無趣了。

辛蒂：謝啦！彼得，如果你負責蒐集整理冰冷的資料，我呢就可以去找一些好照片來做為輔助，強化我們的報告。

德倫：做得好，伙伴們。我們每個星期三和星期天見個面，報告各自的最新進度。

1. division of labor 分工

2. stopped by 中途順便到……

3. reference [ˋrɛfrəns] library 參考資料室

4. relevant [ˋrɛləvənt] *adj.* 切題的；有關連的

5. go-getter [ˋgo͵gɛtɚ] *n.* 有幹勁的人

6. materials [məˋtɪrɪəl] *n.* 材料；資料

7. public speaking 公開演說

8. graphic design 平面設計

9. track down 查出；探知

10. update [͵ʌpˋdet] *v.* 為……補充最新資料

補充單字 In Context CD2  09

stubborn / cooperative 頑固的/合作的

☞ You: Billy is **stubborn**. He only wants to do things his way.

Classmate: Yeah, he doesn't seem to work well in groups and he certainly isn't very **cooperative**.

你： 比利很頑固。他只想照自己的方式做事。

同學： 是呀，他分組的時候表現似乎不是很好，而且他真的不怎麼合作。

handout 講義

Classmate: Let's prepare a **handout** for the class.

☞ You: Good idea. We can include an outline of the main points we're going to make.

同學： 我們幫班上同學準備一份講義吧！

你： 好主意。我們可以在裡面放報告的重點大綱。

rehearse 彩排

Classmate: I think we should **rehearse** our presentation one more time.

☞ You: OK. Pretty soon I'll have it completely memorized.

同學： 我認為我們應該再把報告排練一次。

你： 好的。很快我就會全都背起來了。

---

cite / source 引用／出處

Classmate: Do we need to **cite** our **sources** for all this data?

☞ You: Yes, I think we do.

同學： 我們需要註明所有引用資料的出處嗎？

你： 是的，我想我們得這麼做。

visuals 視覺上的輔助

Classmate: This map is perfect.

☞ You: I agree. But our presentation still needs more **visuals**. I think we should do a slide show.

同學： 這張地圖棒極了。

你： 我同意，但是我們的報告還需要更多視覺上的輔助。我想我們應該要做張投影片。

---

workload 工作量

Classmate: This isn't fair! We agreed to share the **workload**, but I'm doing everything!

☞ You: So you say! I've done twice as much work as you!

同學： 這不公平！我們要平分工作量，但是現在所有的事都是我在做！

你： 那是你說的。我做的是你做的兩倍耶！

allotted 撥出

Classmate:	We've got to cut down our presentation time.
☞ You:	You're right! That took almost an hour, but we're only **allotted** fifteen minutes.

同學：	我們得縮短報告的時間。
你：	沒錯！我們幾乎得用了一個小時，但我們只分配到十五分鐘。

involve 參予

☞ You:	I think our presentation will be more effective if we can **involve** the professor in some way.
Classmate:	But how?

你：	我認為我們的報告如果能想個法子讓教授也軋上一角，就會更精彩。
同學：	但是要怎麼做呢？

audience 觀眾

☞ You:	I think our **audience** was impressed.
TA:	The professor looked really interested. Most of the students were paying attention, too.

你：	我想我們讓觀眾留下了深刻的印象。
助教：	教授看起來很感興趣。大部分的學生也都很專心地在聽。

留學 Survival Kits CD2 10

1 號 法寶 **Public speaking** 公開演說

☞ For many students, the hardest part of a group project is doing the actual presentation. Almost everyone gets a little nervous when they have to speak in front of a group. Some get very nervous indeed. Even if one member of your group feels more comfortable presenting, you'll still benefit if you also do some of the talking. The only way to improve your public-speaking skills is to practice, and group presentations are a valuable opportunity to do just that. Sure you'll be nervous, but if you're well prepared you'll do fine. And even if you don't, you'll have gained valuable experience that will help you do even better next time.

☞ 對很多學生來說,分組報告最困難的一部份是實際發表。當要面對一群人講話時,幾乎每個人都會有些緊張。而有些人真的會感到非常緊張。即使你那一組中有一個人能輕鬆地上台發表,如果你也能講一部份,也會有所收穫。要改善公開演說的技巧,唯一的方法就是練習,而分組報告正是練習的寶貴機會。你當然會緊張,但是如有你有萬全準備,你就會做得很好。即使你沒有做得很好,你也會得到寶貴的經驗,有助於你下一次能做得更好。

2號法寶 Three simple steps to successful presentations
成功發表報告的三步驟

☞ When giving any presentation, there is an old formula that's tough to beat. It's easy to follow, easy to remember, and it really works.

1. Tell'em what you're going to tell'em.
2. Tell'em.
3. Tell'em what you told'em.

Or, in other words, first tell your audience what the main point of your presentation is. Then make your presentation. Finally, review the main points of your presentation.

☞ 在做任何報告時，有一個屢試不爽的不二法門。它不但容易執行，
容易記住，而且很管用。

1. 告訴他們你要告訴他們什麼。
2. 告訴他們。
3. 告訴他們你告訴他們了什麼。

換句話說，一開始先告訴你的聽眾你報告內容的重點。然後做你的
報告。最後，再重述你發表中說過的重點。

3 號 法 寶 **6 Tips for a successful PowerPoint slide presentation**
做好成功的 PowerPoint 投影簡報六要訣

1. 從前言的投影片開始。它應包括題目，和報告人的姓名。

   • "Today I'll be talking about . . ."
   • "I've prepared a slide presentation . . ."

2. 接下來的投影片要把你報告中的主題列成綱要。

   • "I want to make the following main points."
   • "This slide provides a preview..."

3. 不要把你簡報的全文放到投影片上，只需秀出你的要點就可以了。使用轉折語氣來強調要點。

   • "The main point is that . . ."
   • "In addition . . ."
   • "Furthermore . . ."
   • "I'd like to add . . ."

4. 別快速的翻動投影片。讓聽眾有足夠的時間去看投影片。使用簡短的句子來介紹投影片，然後暫停一會兒讓聽眾有足夠的時間吸收視訊。

- "This next slide deals with . . ."
- "This slide focuses on . . ."

5. 要確保你的投影片整齊清楚，可以讓每位聽眾都看得見。仔細地校對，仔細檢查文法、拼法、標點符號和大寫。

- "Is everyone able to see clearly?"
- "Please let me know if anything on the slides is not clear."
- "Please speak up if . . ."

6. 在你的報告近尾聲時，記得加入一張總結你的主要觀點的投影片，另一張列出你報告中所使用資料的來源。

- "In summary . . ."
- "To conclude . . ."
- "I'll be happy now to answer any questions you may have.
- "Thank you very much for your time and attention."

:::::: Quiz

Complete the dialogue.

**presentation, research, audience, public speaking,
visuals, workload, division of labor, made a plan**

Cindy: I think we're going to get a great grade on our
1_____.

Peter: I agree. It went great.

Cindy: Your 2_____ was very thorough. And the
3_____ really responded to the photos and other
4_____ I selected.

Peter: Darren did a nice job, too. He's so comfortable with
5_____.

Cindy: I was nervous, but that was actually really fun. I feel
pumped!

Peter: Our 6_____ was very efficient. We all shared the
7_____.

Cindy: We 8_____, and we stuck to it.

Peter: We're awesome.

Cindy: I agree.

....

🗂 Answers

1. presentation
2. research
3. audience
4. visuals

5. public speaking
6. division of labor
7. workload
8. made a plan

:::::: *Notes*

Chapter 7

Tests

第 七 章

考試

開學第一天

 CD2 11

Are you ready? 先來一點新生訓練介紹，了解課程基本面……

Students often get extremely nervous around test time, and for good reason. The mid-term and final exam often account for the majority of a final grade. And if getting good grades is important to you, you'll need to have (or quickly develop!) good test-taking skills. Fortunately, there are a few general principles that provide a starting point for successful test preparation. Remember, there's no secret to doing well on tests; you just have to know the material! If you have real interest in the subject and devote yourself to learning one day at a time, all of your hard work will be done before test day.

一到考試學生就會變得格外緊張，這是很合理的，因為期中考和期末考通常佔了期末成績的絕大部分。如果得到好成績對你來說很重要的話，你就必須要具備（或是快點培養！）好的應試技巧。幸運的是，有幾個大的原則，可以提供作為成功準備考試的開始。記住，要考得好沒有訣竅；你就是得熟悉教材內容。如果你對這個科目真的有興趣，而且每一天都很專心學習，所有辛勤的工作都會在考試日之前告一段落。

進入狀況

📁 About the Final Exam 期末考相關事項

Pol Sci 103 — Intro to International Relations

Zabignew Mittleman, TA

The Format of the Final Exam

One week before the final exam, Prof. Hardt will hand out a list of fifteen essay topics. From this list, Prof. Hardt will choose four topics for the final. You need to respond to two of them during the exam. You'll have two hours. Bring a blue book and two blue or black pens. Notes are not allowed.

Test Preparation Tips

1. Don't stay up all night cramming. It'll do more harm than good.
2. Talk to students who have taken the class in previous years to get a feel for the kinds of questions the teacher is likely to choose. Form study groups, divide up the questions, and share possible responses.
3. Ask the professor for advice on how to prepare. Prof. Hardt has office hours this week and next week, and he will be happy to point you in the right direction.
4. Attend the review session. These will be held by all the TAs (including me), probably a day or two before the test. I'll let you know exactly when and where as soon as we've booked the room.
5. Review the readings and your notes for a short time every day, starting from today. Seriously. Don't wait till the last minute.

政治學 103 — 國際關係概論

薩比紐・米特曼助教

期末考試形式

期末考的前一週，哈德特教授會發一張印有十五題申論題的一覽表。哈德特教授將從表中選出四個題目作為期末試題。在考試的時候，你需要回答其中兩題。你會有兩個小時的時間。請攜帶一本作答用的藍皮簿以及兩支藍色或黑色的筆。不可以帶筆記。

考試準備小訣竅

1. 不要整晚熬夜臨時抱佛腳，那樣做的壞處多過於好處。
2. 跟以前修過這門課的學生聊一聊，了解一下老師可能會選擇的題目類型。組成讀書會，分頭做題目，並且分享可能的答案。
3. 向教授請教如何準備考試。哈德特教授這星期和下星期都有辦公時間，而且他會樂於指點你正確的方向。
4. 來參加複習班。大約在考試的前一、兩天，會由所有的助教（包括我）共同召開。只要我們預約好了教室，就會讓各位知道切確的時間和地點。
5. 從今天起，每天花一點時間複習要讀的書和你的筆記。說真的，不要等到最後一分鐘。

 ○ 。

CD2 12

📁 Exam Preparation Strategies

Cindy and Peter are hanging out at the gym complaining about their upcoming test.

Cindy: I can't believe we have to write two essays for our final exam!

Peter: Did you expect calculus problems? Cindy, it's an international relations class.

Cindy: I know. It's just that writing [1] <u>stresses me out</u>.

Peter: At least we can choose which essay topics to respond to.

Cindy: Have you decided how you're going to prepare?

Peter: Not yet. I'm writing some notes on a couple different themes. I'm going to be well prepared for this test. No [2] <u>cramming</u>!

Cindy: I think I'm actually going to write an essay or two in advance. Kind of like a [3] <u>practice run</u>.

Peter: Me too. I mean, why not?

Cindy: And I'm going to memorize an opening sentence for each of the topics. If I [4] <u>panic</u>, at least I'll be able to get started.

Peter: Except if you panic, you might forget it.

Cindy: Don't say that! I'm going to have a good, strong first sentence that [5] <u>gets right to the point</u> and I'm not going to forget it.

Peter: Right. And you'll follow up with a [6] <u>fluent</u>, concise essay. You won't try to say too much.

Cindy: I'll use examples to illustrate my key points and connect them with smooth transitions. My [7] <u>summary</u> will be clear and concise. I'll leave enough time to review and correct any [8] <u>misspellings</u> or [9] <u>awkward</u> sentences. My essay is going to be extraordinary!

Peter: And you'll get an A+!

Cindy: Now you're talking!

📂 考試準備策略

辛蒂和彼得在健身房裡抱怨即將到來的考試。

辛蒂：我真不敢相信我們期末考得寫兩題申論題！

彼得：難道妳期待的是微積分的計算題嗎？辛蒂，這堂課可是國際關係耶。

辛蒂：我知道。只是寫作讓我覺得壓力太大了。

彼得：至少我們可以選擇題目來回答。

辛蒂：你決定好要怎麼準備了嗎？

彼得：還沒有。我在做幾個不同題目的筆記。我會做好這個考試的萬全準備。絕不臨時抱佛腳！

辛蒂：我想我真的要事先寫一或兩篇文章。就像熱身賽一樣。

彼得：我也是。我的意思是，這沒什麼不好的。

辛蒂：而且我要把回答每一題的第一句話背起來。如果我慌了手腳，至少我還能起個頭。

彼得：只是如果妳真的慌了手腳，妳還是可能會忘記。

辛蒂：別說那種話！我要想出很棒、很有力，而且能一下就切中要點的第一句話，而且我一定不會忘記。

彼得：是呀！然後妳就會接著寫出一篇流暢、簡潔的文章。妳不會試圖寫太多。

辛蒂：我會舉例子來說明我的主要論點，而且用流暢的轉折詞把它們連結起來。我的總結會是清楚簡潔的。我會留下足夠的時間來檢查、訂正拼字錯誤或不順暢的句子。我的文章將會超棒！

彼得：然後妳會得到一個 A+!

辛蒂：這還差不多！

必備字彙 ○。

1. **stress me out** 讓我壓力太大

2. **cramming** [ˋkræmɪŋ] *n.* 填鴨式的用功；臨時抱佛腳

3. **practice run** 熱身賽

4. **panic** [ˋpænɪk] *v.* 驚慌失措

5. **get right to the point** 直接切中要點

6. **fluent** [ˋfluənt] *adj.* 流暢的

7. **summary** [ˋsʌmərɪ] *n.* 總摘要

8. **misspelling** [mɪsˋspɛlɪŋ] *n.* 拼錯

9. **awkward** [ˋɔkwəd] *adj.* 拙劣的；不順暢的

Take a Break

討論 II.  ○。

CD2 13

📁 Complaining About Grades

Peter catches Cindy after their tests are returned.

Peter: How'd you do on your essay, Cindy?

Cindy: OK. I got an 83 — a B. How about you?

Peter: B minus. I don't know what happened. I thought I would do better.

Cindy: [1] Whoever heard of grading an essay exam [2] on a curve?

Peter: That's just how Professor Hardt does it, I guess. It makes it hard for those of us who are still learning English.

Cindy: Yeah. Oh, well. [3] Multiple-choice tests are easier, but I feel like I learned a lot preparing for this test.

Peter: That's true. Me too. And we did better than a lot of people who are native speakers. That's pretty good, I guess.

Cindy: And Professor Hardt wrote some very [4] thoughtful [5] comments on my exam. I haven't really felt like studying them yet, but I will soon.

Peter: [6] All things considered, I guess we did pretty well. Still, I'm looking forward to my Geography [7] quiz this afternoon. It's a [8] true-or-false test!

抱怨成績

考卷發回來之後彼得找辛蒂聊了聊。

彼得：你的申論寫得如何，辛蒂？

辛蒂：還可以。我得了 83 分——是個 B。你呢？

彼得：B 減。我不知道怎麼回事。我原以為會考得好一點。

辛蒂：你聽過有人用常態分佈來打申論分數的嗎？

彼得：我想哈德特教授就是那樣做的。那對我們這些還在學習英文的人
　　　來說就難了。

辛蒂：是啊。喔，算了。多重選擇就容易多了，不過我覺得在準備這次
　　　考試的時候學到了不少。

彼得：那倒是真的。我也是。而且我們比其他很多本國人考得好。我想
　　　這點還不錯。

辛蒂：而且哈德特教授在我的考卷上寫了一些關切的評語。我還沒有真
　　　的想仔細看，不過很快就會。

彼得：整個想一想，我想我們表現得蠻好的。儘管如此，我現在正期待
　　　著下午的地理小考。是考是非題！

○。

1 Whoever heard of... 誰聽說過……

2 on a curve 常態分佈

3 multiple-choice test 考選擇題的考試

4 thoughtful [ˋθɔtfəl] *adj.* 體貼的；關切的

5 comment [ˋkɑmɛnt] *n.* 評論

6 All things considered 整個想一想……

7 quiz [kwɪz] *n.* 小考

8 true-or-false test 考是非題的考試

補充單字 In Context CD2 14

to pull an all-nighter 開夜車

☞ You: You look like you just **pulled an all-nighter**.

Classmates: I did. I was cramming for my history exam.

你：   你看起來像是開了整晚的夜車。

同學：   我是呀！我拚命在背歷史考試的東西。

---

state / indecipherable 陳述／令人不解的

☞ You: I tried to **state** my position as clearly as possible, but the professor said my essay was
"puzzling and pretty much **indecipherable**."

Classmates: Bummer.

你：   我嘗試盡可能地把我的論點陳述清楚，但是教授說我的
申論「教人困惑，而且非常難以理解」。

同學：   真是糟糕！

performance on a test 考試的表現

☞ You:　　　Are you aware that your diet can affect your **performance on a test**?

Classmates: I like to eat candy and drink coffee to get pumped for a test. Is that what you mean?

你：　　　你知道飲食會影響你在考試時的表現嗎？

同學：　　我喜歡在考試前吃糖果和喝咖啡來振作精神。你說的是這個嗎？

---

strategic 策略的

☞ You:　　　I take a **strategic** approach to answering test questions. I always start with the easy ones.

Classmates: Good plan. That way, you build your confidence at the beginning.

你：　　　我採取策略性的方式答考題。我都從簡單的開始寫。

同學：　　好方法。這樣一來，你從一開始就建立了信心。

proofread 校勘

☞ You: I have an essay exam tomorrow. Yuck.

Classmates: Make sure you leave time at the end to **proofread** your work. Professors appreciate a tidy essay.

你：   我明天有個考申論題的考試。真討厭。

同學：   記得要在最後留時間檢查你寫的內容。教授們喜歡井然有序的文章。

---

penalized / guess （考試的）處罰：扣分／猜測

☞ You: If you're not **penalized** for wrong answers, just **guess** on the ones you don't know.

Classmates: Don't worry. I'm good at guessing.

你：   如果答錯不扣分的話，不會答的就用猜的吧。

同學：   別擔心，我是很會猜的。

open book 可翻書的

☞ You: All the tests in my American History class are **open book**.

Classmates: Lucky you.

你： 我在美國歷史那一堂課中所有的考試都可以翻書。

同學： 你真幸運。

---

to burn the midnight oil 熬夜

☞ You: Big test tomorrow?

Classmates: Yeah. I'll be **burning the midnight oil** tonight.

你： 明天有大考嗎？

同學： 對呀！我今晚要挑燈夜戰了。

to ace (a test) 考試得滿分

Classmate: How'd you do on the exam?

☞ You: Great. I **aced** it.

同學： 你考試考得如何？

你： 好極了。我得了 A。

to post results 公佈結果

Classmate: Has Professor King **posted the results** for the midterm yet?

☞ You: Yes. They're posted outside his office. You can also see them online.

同學： 金教授公佈期中考的結果了嗎？

你： 是的。貼在他辦公室的外面。你也可以上網查看。

留學 Survival Kits CD2 15

1 號 法 寶 Mnemonics 記憶法

☞ Mnemonics is a proven technique for improving your memory. The word literally means "memory tool." Mnemonics takes advantage of all of the brain's tools by transforming information into a device, such as an image, formula or rhyme, that makes recall easier. The human brain is designed to evaluate and interpret images, colors, structures, sounds, smells, tastes, touch, positions, emotions and language. When you create a mnemonic, you use your imagination to create, say, a vivid image. It can be anything you can imagine, as long as it is familiar and memorable. You then associate this image with the information you want to remember. A very common type of mnemonic is using the letters in a word or name to stand for a group of things you want to remember. For example, an easy way to remember the colors of the rainbow is to think of a man's name: Roy G. Biv, which stands for Red, Orange, Yellow, Green, Blue, Indigo and Violet. Once you've met Roy, you won't likely forget him.

☞ 記憶術是被證實能用來增進記憶的方法。這個字在字面上是「記憶工具」的意思。記憶術利用腦部的所有工具將資訊轉換成某種方式，例如影像、公式或是韻文等，使我們能夠將事物較容易地記起來。人類頭腦的構造能讓我們去評估並詮釋影像、顏色、結構、聲音、氣味、味道、觸感、位置、情緒以及語言。當你創造一個記憶符號時，就是運用你的想像力去創造，譬如說，一個生動的影像。它可以是任何你能想像得到的東西，只要是熟悉而且容易記住的。然後你再將這個影像跟你想要記住的資訊作連結。常見的記憶符號是用單字或名字中的字母來代表一組你想記住的東西。例如，要記住彩虹顏色的一個簡單的方法是，記住一個人的名字：Roy G. Biv，它代表紅色 (Red)、橘色 (Orange)、黃色 (Yellow)、綠色 (Green)、藍色 (Blue)、靛青色 (Indigo)、以及紫色 (Violet)。一旦你認識了 Roy，你就不可能忘記他。

2號 法寶 Emergency Cramming 臨時抱佛腳

☞ OK. You should have done the readings. You should have attended all the lectures. You should have been reviewing your notes. But you didn't. Now it's test time. Obviously, you're not going to give a superlative performance. But if there is still some time left, you can use it wisely. You need to prioritize your goals. You need to cram. If your test is an in-class essay, you can try the following approach. Identify a few key ideas that will likely be covered on the test. Use a sheet of paper for each concept and write—in your own words—a definition or an explanation for each concept. Don't use your notes or textbook. Then go back and compare your "answers" with your notes and textbook. Revise them if necessary. Stack your pages in order of importance and review them as you walk around. If you have time, add three or four more pages and ideas. That's probably enough. You can only cram so much into your brain on short notice. Good luck. You're going to need it.

☞ 好，你現在應該已經把書讀完了。你應該已經每一堂課都去上了。你應該已經複習好你的筆記了。但是你卻都沒有。現在要考試了。顯然你將不會有特優的表現。不過如有你還有一點時間，你可以妥善地利用。你需要把目標的優先順序理出來。你需要臨時抱佛腳。如果你的考試是隨課申論，你可以試試看以下的方法。找出一些可能會考的關鍵概念。把每個概念的定義或是解釋用自己的話寫在紙上，一個概念一張。不要使用你的筆記和課本。然後回頭把你的「答案」和你的筆記、課本作個比較，先作必要的改寫，再依重要性的高低排序把它們疊起來，一邊走一邊複習。如果你有時間的話，再增加三、四頁多寫幾個概念。那大概就夠了。在短時間內，你的腦袋也只能擠進這麼多東西了。祝你好運，因為，你將會需要它。

::::::: Quiz

Complete the dialogue.

test performance, panic, all-nighter, cramming, burning the midnight oil, multiple-choice, stressed out, guess

Cindy: I am totally 1_____. I had three midterms today.

Peter: Three? Wow. That's tough.

Cindy: And I wasn't prepared for my biology test. I was up all night 2_____.

Peter: Uh oh. 3_____ time.

Cindy: Luckily, it was a 4_____ test. I had to 5_____ a few times, but I actually was pretty sure of myself on most of the questions.

Peter: I'm not pulling any more 6_____. Last time I tried that, my 7_____ really suffered.

Cindy: I wish I could say the same. But I'm going to be 8_____ again tonight. I have one more test tomorrow.

Peter: If you want, I'll bring you some fresh coffee. That might help.

··

📁 Answers

1. stressed out

2. cramming

3. panic

4. multiple-choice

5. guess

6. all-nighter

7. test performance

8. burning the midnight oil

∷∷∷Notes

Chapter 8

Writing Papers

第 八 章

寫報告

開學第一天

CD2　16

Are you ready? 先來一點新生訓練介紹，了解課程基本面……

Most long written assignments are due at the end of the semester, when you are trying to prepare for your final exams. For this reason, it is advisable that you get an early start on your final papers, especially if they are of a considerable length (10+ pages). It is helpful to prepare a rough outline of your ideas ahead of time, even if you don't have time to flesh out the content. If you've thought through your ideas and prepared a solid outline, you should be able to finish your final papers on time, even if you do procrastinate a little and end up pulling a few all-nighters at the end of the semester.

　　大多數繳交長篇書面報告的截止日期都是在學期末，也就當你在努力準備期末考試的當口。正因如此，建議你要儘早開始著手你的期末報告，尤其是報告的長度相當可觀時（10 頁以上）。即使你沒有時間充實報告的內容，提早將你的想法寫成初步的大綱還是會很有幫助。假使你已經仔細釐清你的想法，而且也寫好確實完整的大綱，就算你的進度有點耽擱導致期末時得趕幾個通宵，你也應該能準時完成你的期末報告。

進入狀況

📂 About Writing Assignment Correction 有關寫作作業批改

Pol Sci 103 – Intro to International Relations
Prof. Jon Hardt

Formatting Guidelines and Editing Symbols

Papers should be between 2,500–3,000 words (10–12 pages, not including the title page) and printed in 12 point Times New Roman. Leave one-inch margins and include your name in the header of every page. Papers will be returned within one week. The following standard editing symbols will help you when you review your paper.

Symbol	Explanation	Example
∧	Insert letter, punctuation or word(s) here	She went to *the* store.
♂	Delete the words or punctuation	They goes there every day.
⌐	Transpose letters or words	Cut up it.
⌗	Start a new paragraph	…ice cream. Like other
≡	Capitalize	vice president Smith
⌒	Delete the space; make one word	Back pack
|	Insert a space	CDROM

政治學 103 —國際關係概論

強·哈德特教授

格式指引和編輯符號

報告應在 2,500 到 3,000 字之間（10 — 12 頁，不包含標題頁），使用 Times New Roman 字體，大小 12 。邊邊留一吋的空白，並將你的名字列於每一頁的頁首。報告會在一週內發回。以下這些標準的編輯符號將能幫助你檢閱你的報告。

Symbol	Explanation	Example
∧	在此插入字母、標點符號或是字。	She went to *the* store.
♂	刪除字或標點符號。	They goes there every day.
ꙅ	把字母或字對調。	Cut up it.
¶	另起一個新的段落。	... ice cream. Like other
≡	大寫。	vice president Smith
⌒	刪除字間的空格；併成一個字。	Back pack
|	插入一個空格。	CDROM

 ○ °

CD2 17

📂 Revising a Paper

Peter and Cindy chat outside the computer lab. They are reading each other's papers.

Peter: So, what do you think? Do you like it?

Cindy: You have some good ideas, but the organization needs some work, I think.

Peter: What do you mean?

Cindy: Well ... it's not clear what your thesis is. And some of the transitions between [1] <u>paragraphs</u> don't really help the paper flow better.

Peter: But I tried to use [2] <u>topic sentences</u>. And I even made an [3] <u>outline</u> before I started writing, just like the teacher suggested.

Cindy: What can I say? Keep revising! OK, your turn. Comments, please!

Peter: Well, I think your [4] <u>content</u> is fine, but your [5] <u>formatting</u> seems a little strange.

Cindy: Do you mean the [6] <u>spacing</u> between lines, or the [7] <u>margins</u>?

Peter: A little of everything, I'm afraid!

Cindy: All right—I think we both had better make a trip to the writing center before we [8] <u>turn these in</u>.

📁 修改報告

彼得和辛蒂在電腦教室外面聊天。他們正在看彼此的報告。

彼得：怎樣，妳覺得如何？妳喜歡嗎？

辛蒂：你有一些很好的想法，不過我認為架構需要再加強。

彼得：妳的意思是──？

辛蒂：嗯……你的論點不太明確。而且有些段落之間的啟承轉折並沒有
讓文章更流暢。

彼得：但是我嘗試用了主題句。而且我甚至在開始寫之前擬了大綱，就
像老師建議的一樣。

辛蒂：我能說些什麼呢？繼續修改吧！好啦，輪到你了。請給我意見
吧！

彼得：嗯，我認為妳的內容沒問題，不過妳的格式似乎有點怪怪的。

辛蒂：你是指行距還是邊邊的留白？

彼得：恐怕都有一點！

辛蒂：好吧──我想我們兩個在把報告交出去之前，最好要先去一趟寫
作教室。

1. **paragraph** [ˈpærəˌgræf] *n.* 段落

2. **topic sentence** [ˈtɑpɪk ˈsɛntəns] *n.* 主題句

3. **outline** [ˈaʊtˌlaɪn] *n.* 大綱

4. **content** [ˈkɑntənt] *n.* 內容

5. **formatting** [ˈfɔrmætɪŋ] *n.* 格式;版面

6. **spacing** [ˈspesɪŋ] *n.* 間格

7. **margin** [ˈmɑrdʒɪn] *n.* 書頁邊的留白

8. **turn in** 遞交(作業)

::::: *Take a Break*

討論 II. ○。

CD2 18

📂 About the Writing Center

Cindy and Peter bump into each other on the campus shuttle.

Cindy: Hey, Peter. I've just been to the writing center. I don't know how I ever [1] <u>got along</u> without that place.

Peter: Did they help you [2] <u>come up with</u> a [3] <u>conclusion</u> for your paper?

Cindy: Yes. And not only that, they showed me how to [4] <u>format</u> my paper so that 6 1/2 pages became 7 1/2 pages.

Peter: Sneaky!

Cindy: Yeah, don't tell anyone.

Peter: I have to say, the writing center is really amazing. They offer good advice about how to really improve your writing, but they also understand your need to [5] <u>get the paper done on time</u>.

Cindy: The best advice they gave me was to [6] <u>start early</u> and write a little bit each day. That way, I won't get too frustrated.

Peter: And you have time for editing and rewriting before your paper is due.

Cindy: There's time for your ideas to develop.

Peter: And you have time to show your paper to someone else for comments and [7] <u>criticism</u>.

Cindy: There's time for [8] <u>proofreading</u>.

Peter: Basically, if you start early, you have time to do a good job.

Cindy: Yeah. Start early. It's brilliant.

📁 關於寫作中心

辛蒂和彼得無意中在校園的接駁公車上相遇。

辛蒂：嘿，彼得。我剛去了寫作教室。我真不知道如果沒有那個地方我
　　　該怎麼辦。

彼得：他們有沒有幫妳想出報告的結論？

辛蒂：有。而且不只如此，他們還教了我怎麼編排我的報告，所以六頁
　　　半就變成了七頁半。

彼得：好詐!

辛蒂：是啊，千萬不要跟別人說。

彼得：我必須得說，寫作教室真是太棒了。他們不但提供改善作文的好
　　　建議，甚至還了解你需要準時完成報告的需求。

辛蒂：他們給我最好的建議是要提早開始，而且每天寫一點。這樣子的
　　　話，我就不會太有挫折感。

彼得：而且在截止期限之前，你還能有時間編輯、修改你的報告。

辛蒂：你就有時間闡述你的概念。

彼得：而且你會有時間將報告拿去請教其他人的意見或批評建議。

辛蒂：也有時間校對。

彼得：基本上，如果你及早開始，就會有時間把報告做好。

辛蒂：是啊。早早開始。真是個妙主意。

必備字彙 ○。

1 **get along** （勉強）應付

2 **come up with** 想出……點子

3 **conclusion** [ˋkənkluʒən] *n.* 結論

4 **format** [ˋfɔrmæt] *v.* 製定版面

5 **get it done on time** 準時完成

6 **start early** 及早開始

7 **criticism** [ˋkrɪtəˏsɪzəm] *n.* 批評

8 **proofreading** [ˋprufridɪŋ] *n.* 校對

●●●補充單字 In Context CD2 🎧 19

footnote / endnote / citation 註腳／文末備註／引文

☞ You: I hate **footnotes**! I can never get the formatting right!

TA: Why don't you use **endnotes** instead? Just put all your **citations** at the end of your paper. Prof. Hardt doesn't care.

你： 我討厭註腳！我永遠也無法把格式弄對！

助教： 你何不用文末備註來代替呢？只要把你所有的引文都放在報告的最後。哈德特教授並不介意。

---

style 文體

☞ You: Should I try to write with any particular **style**?

Professor: Be clear. Be concise. That's it.

你： 我應該採用任何特別的體例嗎？

教授： 只要清楚、簡潔就可以了。

style manual 文體手冊

☞ You: Can you recommend a good **style manual**?

TA: A lot of people say The Chicago Manual of
            Style is the best.

你：   你可以推薦一本好的體例手冊嗎？

助教：   很多人都說「芝加哥體例手冊」是最棒的。

---

quote 引述

Classmate: Why are you **quoting** Elvis Presley in your
            English paper?

☞ You: Keep reading. You'll see.

同學：   你為什麼在你的英文報告中引述貓王的話？

你：   繼續看下去，你就會明白。

quotation 引文

TA: If your paper is too short, try adding a few **quotations**.

☞ You: You're a genius! Why didn't I think of that?

助教： 如果你的報告太短的話，試試增加一些引文。

你： 你真是天才！我怎麼沒想到呢？

---

title 標題

Classmate: How important is it to have a good **title** for your paper?

☞ You: I'm not sure. It can't hurt to have a good one.

同學： 報告有個好標題有多重要呢？

你： 我也不太知道。有個好標題並沒什麼不好。

cut 刪

TA:	I think you should **cut** this paragraph.
☞ You:	You're right. I thought it was interesting, but it belongs in a different paper.

助教：	我認為你應該刪掉這一個段落。
你：	你說的對。我原本覺得這段很有意思，不過它屬於不同篇的報告。

paraphrase 釋義

☞ You:	I think you've plagiarized this from Professor King's book. He's going to notice that for sure.
Classmate:	I'm not plagiarizing. I'm just **paraphrasing** some of his ideas. Read it again and you'll see that I've given him credit.

你：	我認為你這是抄襲自金教授的著作。他一定會注意到的。
同學：	我沒有抄襲。我只是把他一部份的概念加以釋義。你再看一次，就知道我還是把功勞歸於他。

:::::: *Take a Break*

留學 Survival Kits CD2 20

1 號 法 寶 **The Secret to Good Writing** 成功寫作的秘訣

☞ The secret to good writing is rewriting. If you were to ask a professional writer how to improve your writing, he or she would probably say something that boils down to this: Revise, revise, and revise. If you want to write a good paper, start early. Because writing requires so much energy and concentration, it's best to work only a few hours at a time. If you write your paper the night before it's due, you won't have any time at all for rewriting. Writing can be a painfully difficult chore, but if you persist, you'll soon achieve good results.

☞ 寫好文章的秘訣就是重寫。如果你問一個職業作家關於改進寫作之道,他或她可能會總結一句話:修改、修改、再修改。如果你想寫好一篇報告,及早開始。因為寫作需要非常多的精力和專注力,所以最好一次只寫幾個鐘頭。如果你在截止的前一晚才寫報告,你根本不會有任何時間做修改。寫作可以是件費力又困難的苦差事,不過如果你能堅持下去,很快就會做出好的成果。

2 號 法 寶 **Dissertation** 博士論文

☞ If you're going to continue your education and pursue a doctoral degree, you'll have to be prepared to do some serious writing. You will have to write a dissertation. A dissertation is a book-length paper that doctoral candidates write to show their mastery of a field. Most dissertations require extensive, original research and concise writing. Some dissertations are later revised and submitted for publication as a book.

☞ 如果你要繼續深造攻讀博士學位，就必須有認真把文章寫好的準備。你將得撰寫博士論文。博士論文相當於一本書的長度，博士候選人撰寫論文來展現他們對某個領域的精通。大部分的博士論文需要有廣泛、具原創性的研究，以及簡潔的文字。有些博士論文以後會被加以修改，付梓成書。

3 號 法 寶 **Brainstorming** 腦力激盪

☞ Brainstorming is a way to quickly generate a lot of ideas for solving a specific problem. Here's how it works. Just sit down and start dreaming up ideas. They'll come slowly at first. Jot them down, no matter how bad they seem at first. This is the critical point: do not be critical of any idea that comes! Just write it down and move on to the next one. Your mind will begin to loosen up and the ideas will begin to flow more readily. Write them all down! Do not try to differentiate between good ideas and bad ones. There are no bad ideas yet! A bad idea may lead to a good idea. A bad idea may, upon further reflection, turn out to be a good idea. Only after your brainstorming session is over should you evaluate the quality of the ideas that you came up with. If it works, there will be several that are worth keeping.

☞ 腦力激盪是能快速激發許多點子來解決特定問題的方法。以下是它進行的方式。先坐下來，讓你的想像力開始馳騁。一開始的時候靈感會慢慢地才來。不論一開始時它們顯得有多糟糕，都把它們記下來。這是關鍵所在：不要對想到的點子太過挑剔。直接把它寫下來，然後繼續想下一個。你的頭腦會開始放鬆，靈感也會更快速地湧現。把它們全都寫下來！不要嘗試去分好點子和爛點子。此時還沒有任何點子是糟糕的！一個爛點子也許會讓你找到好點子。一個爛點子也許在經過進一步省思之後會變成一個好點子。應該在腦力激盪時間結束後，再來評估所想到的點子的好壞。如果成功的話，將會有好幾個值得保留的點子。

4 號 法 寶 Citations 引用文獻

☞ Make sure you attribute the sources of your ideas and theories. Your professor or academic department will offer some guidelines about how you should cite your sources. The most prominent conventions for citations are APA (American Psychological Association), Chicago (from the Chicago Manual of Style), MLA (Modern Language Association) and Turabian. The APA style is used in psychology, education and other social sciences. The MLA style is used in literature, arts and humanities. The Turabian style of citing sources was designed for students to use in any subject. The Chicago style is used in books and magazines, while the AP style is used in many newspapers. The various styles are very similar to one another. But when it comes to citations, the details are important. Getting the spacing right matters, for example. Refer to one of the citation guides mentioned above for the exact details.

☞ 要確定你交代了概念和理論的出處。你的教授或是系上會提供一些該如何註明文獻出處的準則。最有名的引用格式標準慣例有 APA（美國心理學會）、芝加哥格式（出自芝加哥論文格式）、MLA（現代語言學會）以及 Turabian 格式。 APA 格式用在心理學、教育以及其他社會科學。 MLA 格式用於文學、藝術、和人文學科。Turabian 引用文獻的格式被設計成能適用於任何學科的學生。芝加哥格式用在書籍與雜誌，而 AP（Associated Press 美聯社）此格式用於大部分的報紙上。這些不同的格式彼此很相近。不過涉及到文獻的引用，細節就很重要了。比方說，使用正確的行距就很要緊。切確的細節請參考上述文獻引用指南之一。

::::::: *Quiz*

Complete the dialogue.

citations, title, start early, getting it done on time,
coming up with, style manual, endnotes, proofreading,
thinking up

Peter: The hardest part about writing a paper is 1_____ a good idea.

Cindy: For me, the hardest part is 2_____. I hate deadlines.

Peter: Whenever I have a deadline, I 3_____. That way I don't get too stressed out.

Cindy: Easier said than done. Another thing I hate are 4_____. I never know how to do them right. My psych professor deducted points because I didn't get the spacing in my 5_____ right!

Peter: Do you have a 6_____? I use the Chicago Manual of Style.

Cindy: Yeah, but some of the professors want you to use a different style.

Peter: True. It's really confusing sometimes.

Cindy: One thing I don't mind is 7_____. At least then, most of the hard work has already been done.

Peter: My favorite job is 8_____ a 9_____ for my paper after it is completely done.

···

📁 Answers

1. coming up with

2. getting it done on time

3. start early

4. citations (or endnotes)

5. endnotes (or citations)

6. style manual

7. proofreading

8. thinking up

9. title

:::::: *Notes*

●●●● 英美用語對照

📁 食

British	American	Explanations/Examples
stout/bitter/ lager	beer/draft	stout 與 bitter 皆為黑啤，stout 比 bitter 濃，顏色較深，甚至 為黑，lager 呈黃至金黃色澤。
aubergine	eggplant	茄子
bangers and mash	sausages and mashed potatoes	香腸與馬鈴薯泥是 pub 菜單上 常見的組合餐點
biscuit	cookie/cracker	cookie 是指美式甜口味的餅乾； cracker 是美式鹹的口味的餅 乾。
butty	sandwich	三明治。最受歡迎的一種為 chip butty，請見以下說明。
crisps	potato chips	洋芋片
chips	fried potatoes/ french fries	在英國薯條通常與魚排一起搭 配吃，稱為 fish and chips。 或是夾配在三明治當中一起吃 ，稱為 chip butty。英國的薯 條通常較厚且寬。
gateau	cake	gateau 原為法文蛋糕的說法， 但英國在商品上多沿用。

📁 衣

British	American	Explanations/Examples
macintosh	raincoat	雨衣
jumper	sweater	毛衣
waistcoat	vest	對美國人而言，vest 指穿在西裝外套下、襯衫外的背心，英國人稱其為 waistcoat；vest 對英國人而言是指內衣背心。

📁 教育

British	American	Explanations/Examples
tutor	instructor	Tutor 在英國大學裡為個別指導一定數目學生的教師，通常由博士班研究生擔任。其角色相當於美國大學裡的 instructor 講師。但有時 instructor 可泛指在大學授課的教師，包括 professor 教授、assistant professor 助教授、lecturer 講師等。
postgraduate student	graduate student	大學畢業後的研究生
marks	grades	在英國成績是以分數(marks)計，在美國則以等級(grades)計。
viva	orals	指英國博士班論文的口試。Viva 是拉丁文 viva voce 的簡寫，意思為" with the living voice"。

📂 常見物件名稱與地名

British	American	Explanations/Examples
bin	trash can	垃圾桶
petrol	gasoline	汽油
the first floor	the second floor	對英國人而言，first floor 指建築物的第二層樓，即美國人所謂的 second floor。第一層樓在英國稱為 ground floor。
flat	apartment	公寓
lift	elevator	電梯
loo	toilet	廁所
cinema/theatre	theater	在英國看電影 (film) 的地方稱為 cinema；欣賞戲劇的地方稱為 theatre。在美國欣賞電影 (movie) 與戲劇的地方皆稱為 theater。

📁 交通、衡量與錢的使用

British	American	Explanations / Examples
single / return	one-way / round-trip	單程與來回票。
queue	line	排隊的隊伍
A pint of beer	A beer	在英國酒吧裡，啤酒是以 pint（品脫）為計量單位來賣的，比如，"A pint of Tetley's"，或 "A half of Boddington's." 在美國則指「一瓶或一杯啤酒」。
quid	buck	quid 為英國錢幣單位 pound（英鎊）較口語的用法；相對的，在美國 buck 則為 dollar 的口語用法。

登峰美語 留學考試系列

出國深造找登峰，留學考試快易通！

TOEFL

班別	課程規劃
實力突破班	42堂正課+9次模考+15堂專題
全修班	36堂正課+9次模考+15堂專題
精修班	30堂正課+7次模考+15堂專題
假日班	30堂正課+7次模考+15堂專題

GMAT

班別	課程規劃
實力突破班	64堂正課+10次模考+15堂專題
全修班	56堂正課+10次模考+15堂專題
精修班	40堂正課+6次模考+15堂專題
假日班	56堂正課+10次模考+15堂專題
模考班	40堂正課+6次模考+15堂專題

GRE

班別	課程規劃
實力突破班	46堂正課+22堂字彙專題+10次模考+15堂專題
全修班	46堂正課+22堂字彙專題+10次模考+15堂專題
精修班	42堂正課+16堂字彙專題+8次模考+15堂專題

SAT

驚讚師資：
【字彙】高天華　【閱讀】王靖　【數學】蘇杭
【題型介紹／模考字彙講解】馬翎
【文法／修辭／寫作】李維
精選教材：
・ETS原版教材
・名師精編SAT講義
★精妙課程於暑期密集開班

國家圖書館出版品預行編目資料

會話震撼教育. 留學課堂篇 = Conversation
Boosters. Classes / Mark Hammons 作
－－初版. －－臺北市；貝塔語言，2005〔民94〕
面；　　公分

ISBN 957-729-474-X（平裝附光碟片）

1. 英國語言－會話

805.188　　　　　　　　　　　　　　　　93020450

會話震撼教育——留學課堂篇
Conversation Boosters — Classes

作　　者／ Mark Hammons
總 編 審／王復國
譯　　者／陳宥琳
執行編輯／杜文田

出　　版／貝塔語言出版有限公司
地　　址／台北市 100 館前路 12 號 11 樓
電　　話／(02)2314-2525
傳　　真／(02)2312-3535
郵　　撥／ 19493777 貝塔出版有限公司
客服專線／ (02)2314-3535
客服信箱／ btservice@betamedia.com.tw

總 經 銷／時報文化出版企業股份有限公司
地　　址／桃園縣龜山鄉萬壽路二段 351 號
電　　話／ (02) 2306-6842

出版日期／ 2005 年 1 月初版一刷
定　　價／ 350 元
ISBN ： 957-729-474-X

Conversation Boosters — Classes
Copyright 2005 by Beta Multimedia Publishing

喚醒你的英文語感 ！

折後釘好，直接寄回即可！

100 台北市中正區館前路12號11樓

 貝塔語言出版 收
Beta Multimedia Publishing

 寄件者住址 □□□

![BS] 貝塔語言出版
Beta Multimedia Publishing

讀者服務專線（02）2314-3535　　讀者服務傳真（02）2312-35

客戶服務信箱 btservice@betamedia.com.tw

www.betamedia.com.tw

謝謝您購買本書！！

貝塔語言擁有最優良之英文學習書籍，為提供您最佳的英語學習資訊，您可填妥此表後寄回（免貼郵票）將可不定期收到本公司最新發行書訊及活動訊息！

姓名：＿＿＿＿＿＿＿＿＿＿　性別：□男 □女　生日：＿＿＿年＿＿＿月＿＿＿日

電話：(公)＿＿＿＿＿＿＿＿＿(宅)＿＿＿＿＿＿＿＿＿(手機)＿＿＿＿＿＿＿＿

電子信箱：＿＿＿＿＿＿＿＿＿＿＿＿＿＿＿＿＿＿

學歷：□高中職含以下　□專科　□大學　□研究所含以上

職業：□金融　□服務　□傳播　□製造　□資訊　□軍公教　□出版
　　　□自由　□教育　□學生　□其他

職級：□企業負責人　□高階主管　□中階主管　□職員　□專業人士

1.您購買的書籍是？＿＿＿＿＿＿＿＿＿＿＿＿＿＿

2.您從何處得知本產品？(可複選)
　　　□書店 □網路 □書展 □校園活動 □廣告信函 □他人推薦 □新聞報導 □其他

3.您覺得本產品價格：
　　　□偏高 □合理 □偏低

4.請問目前您每週花了多少時間學英語？
　　　□ 不到十分鐘 □ 十分鐘以上，但不到半小時 □ 半小時以上，但不到一小時
　　　□ 一小時以上，但不到兩小時 □ 兩個小時以上 □ 不一定

5.通常在選擇語言學習書時，哪些因素是您會考慮的？
　　　□ 封面 □ 內容、實用性 □ 品牌 □ 媒體、朋友推薦 □ 價格□ 其他＿＿＿＿

6.市面上您最需要的語言書種類為？
　　　□ 聽力 □ 閱讀 □ 文法 □ 口說 □ 寫作 □ 其他＿＿＿＿＿

7.通常您會透過何種方式選購語言學習書籍？
　　　□ 書店門市 □ 網路書店 □ 郵購 □ 直接找出版社 □ 學校或公司團購
　　　□ 其他＿＿＿＿＿＿

8.給我們的建議：＿＿＿＿＿＿＿＿＿＿＿＿＿＿＿＿
＿＿＿＿＿＿＿＿＿＿＿＿＿＿＿＿＿＿＿＿＿＿＿＿＿

喚醒你的英文語感！

Get a Feel for English !

喚醒你的英文語感 ！

Get a Feel for English !